HIGH RISK

Visit us at www.boldstrokesbooks.com

Praise for JLee Meyer's Novels

"*Forever Found*...neatly combines hot sex scenes, humor, engaging characters, and an exciting story."—*MegaScene*

In *First Instinct*, "Meyer does a terrific job at developing the espionage storyline and keeping the reader wondering where the next plot twist will lead. Well-developed characters and swift storytelling make this a wonderful read; I couldn't stop turning the pages."—*Lambda Book Report*

"Meyer's heroines are quirky, funny, and so very good together that you can't visualize them apart. Between the multi-dimensional characters with their genuine virtues and flaws, a plot you won't have figured out from the beginning, and a most satisfying conclusion, *First Instinct* leaves readers sated but anxious for more."—*Midwest Book Review*

In *Rising Storm*, "Meyer has given her readers an exciting roller coaster of a ride...This is a book readers will not be able to put down. Be sure to leave a solid block of time with no interruptions!"—*Just About Write*

"*Hotel Liaison* is a tightly written novel with page turning action...This is a great read with a cast of characters that are ideal for a sequel."—*Just About Write*

By the Author

Forever Found

First Instinct

Rising Storm

Hotel Liaison

High Risk

High Risk

by

JLee Meyer

2010

HIGH RISK

ISBN 10:1-60282-136-4
ISBN 13: 978-1-60282-136-1

This Trade Paperback Original Is Published By
Bold Strokes Books, Inc.
P.O. Box 249
Valley Falls, NY 12185

First Edition: February 2010

THIS IS A WORK OF FICTION. NAMES, CHARACTERS, PLACES, AND INCIDENTS ARE THE PRODUCT OF THE AUTHOR'S IMAGINATION OR ARE USED FICTITIOUSLY. ANY RESEMBLANCE TO ACTUAL PERSONS, LIVING OR DEAD, BUSINESS ESTABLISHMENTS, EVENTS, OR LOCALES IS ENTIRELY COINCIDENTAL.

Credits
Editors: Shelley Thrasher and Stacia Seaman
Production Design: Stacia Seaman
Cover Design by Sheri (graphicartist2020@hotmail.com)

Acknowledgments

Shelley Thrasher, our third editing venture. Thank you so much for your time, keen eye, and gentle corrections. As always, much appreciated.

Stacia Seaman, what would we do without you?

Sister and brother authors, you are a delight and inspiration.

Lisa Girolami, you directed me toward some research sites that were most helpful. Hope I did it right.

The staff and volunteers of BSB, you are awesome.

Sheri, Most Venerable Cover Designer, thank you yet again.

Radclyffe, thank you for the opportunity to learn from and be part of such an outstanding group of individuals.

Cheryl, thank you for your feedback and ideas. You know how much I appreciate it.

To the readers, you are why we keep writing. Thank you for your support.

Dedication

Faith is a knowledge within the heart,
beyond the reach of proof.
—Kahlil Gibran

For Cheryl—My faith, my heart, my proof

PROLOGUE

"What are you doing here? I'm calling security."

Dasher Pate squeezed her eyes shut. It had been only a matter of time before Joe Alder showed up to once again shred the fabric of her life. She released the hand she'd been holding, the hand she'd been longing to hold for what seemed like forever, and stood to face him. The machines and tubes attached to Kate Hoffman remained impassive, although Dasher thought the beep on the heart monitor sped up when their connection was severed. Wishful thinking.

"I just stopped by to see how she was." Why was she kowtowing to this man? She wasn't doing anything wrong. "I heard she had an accident on the set. She's asleep, doesn't even know I'm here."

Alder, a short, squat man in his forties, clenched his ever-present unlit cigar in his teeth. "She never will, either. Who let you in?" His small, almost black eyes glittered like marbles as he scanned the area, probably looking for someone to fire. He always appeared sweaty to Dasher, like he was one cheeseburger away from a heart attack.

"No one. I simply walked in. Don't worry, Joe. I'm not here trying to steal your biggest client. I just…needed to see she was okay. I'll leave."

"Isn't your mother in this hospital? What is it this time, too many Prozac combined with a fifth of vodka?" Tobacco-stained teeth were visible around the damned cigar, his enjoyment of Dasher's pain evident.

"My mother is none of your business. I said I was leaving. Maybe you should worry about letting Ms. Hoffman try such dangerous stunts. She's lucky she only tore up her knee and got a concussion."

That must have been the final straw, because Joe was chomping so fast on the cigar it looked like he was getting ready to either swallow it or spit it at her. "Get your bulldyke ass out of this room. She's my client and I tell her what's good for her career. I don't need your fucking opinion. You'll never get her away from me, so I'd advise you to stop trying."

Shaking her head, Dasher stared at Alder. "What's the point of even trying to talk to you?" She couldn't believe this poor excuse for a human being was Kate Hoffman's agent. What kind of lies did he tell Kate to get her to suddenly renege on their promise and sign with him? She'd probably never know.

She left the room and searched the hall for the elevator. Her mother would need her to be there when she woke up. Her dad refused to leave his set, so here she was again, right in the middle.

Her childhood had prepared her perfectly to be the middleperson. No wonder she chose to be a talent agent rather than a part of the stunt-work industry in which her father was hugely successful. She was so accustomed to placating and maneuvering to get peace and quiet that it was second nature for her to soothe egos and manipulate outcomes to get the best for her clients. To survive.

She'd been on her way to the hospital when she heard the news that Kate had been injured and brought to the same location. Breaking every traffic law to get there, she had to check on Kate. She'd had three whole minutes with her before Alder showed up.

Five years and she still had to do it. Had to worry about Kate. The woman had signed with someone else, was straight, and would rarely even look at her if they were at the same function, but Dasher was learning that some things didn't change.

Evidently her feelings for Kate Hoffman were in that category.

Chapter One

"Oh, no. No, no, no." Kate watched with irritation as a white stretch limousine pulled to a stop in front of the Hotel Liaison. That meant her limo would be behind them, *second*. What if whoever was in there was more famous? What if no one paid attention to her when she exited her car? This was a potential disaster.

"Driver, please take me to Neiman Marcus on Union Square. I have to pick up something I forgot to pack."

"Yes, ma'am. If you want, I can get it for you." The woman deftly maneuvered around the parked limousine and continued to the department store, stopped in front, and sprinted to open Kate's door.

"Thank you. I'll only be a few minutes." *Long enough to avoid running into the occupants of that damned limo and pick up a few guaranteed fans for my arrival.* She'd have to have a word with Laurel about warning her when another celebrity might be arriving.

By the time her car glided to the front of the hotel, the white limo was gone and she was confident that she would be suitably surrounded by fans when she got out. She'd been spotted at Neiman's and had mentioned where she'd be staying. Good publicity for Hotel Liaison, too. The stir would probably thrill Laurel, and Kate really did need the cashmere cardigan she'd just bought, since she'd forgotten her favorite sweater. San Francisco was usually much cooler than Los Angeles, and the trade on jackets, sweatshirts, and sweaters for unaware tourists and even savvy visitors like her was brisk.

On cue, a small crowd of autograph seekers and curious onlookers, even a couple of men taking photos, appeared around her. Her liveried driver looked sharp opening the door and offering her hand for Kate to make a graceful exit, always a trick in a stretch limo. An elegant Vera Wang dress almost the color of her unusual green eyes, with a hint of her generous cleavage, helped rivet her admirers' attention. Thick blond hair worn past her shoulders and perfectly applied makeup enhanced the picture that fans worldwide drooled over. Wearing tall, strappy, sexy heels that made her nudge six feet in height, she was larger than life. But that was the idea. However, no amount of fan approval would stop her feet from killing her. She hated those damned shoes.

Sometimes being famous was worth it and sometimes it sucked. Kate Hoffman ignored the ache in her knee and smiled luminously at the crowd of autograph seekers. She signed, stood beside them for photos, did not allow what she now suspected were the professional photographers to elbow in front of some of the shyer people, and then waved good-bye as she gingerly made her way to the hotel entrance.

The final three fans scuttled down the street laughing and shouting to each other about their good fortune. This was one of her favorite things to do, because most fans were so adoring and nice. They filled her life with pleasure. Although the photographers had been rude, they seemed to have backed off. Perhaps because the doorkeeper had put herself squarely between them and Kate.

She gave the imposing employee of the soon-to-be-open

Hotel Liaison a small grin as she walked inside, trying not to favor her leg. Her sister Laurel was at the front desk standing behind a seated young woman who was earnestly studying the computer screen in front of her. The hotel had invited some guests to beta test its accommodations, and Kate was among them.

Actually, she'd been there a lot recently. Having injured her knee while shooting her most recent movie, she had endured the pain with ice packs and wraps in order to finish filming. Luckily, before the accident she'd completed most of the scenes that required running, escaping, and undressing.

Laurel insisted she take some time to regroup and rehab the knee in San Francisco, saying she could stay on the Elysium private floors and no one would bother her. Kate had already volunteered to be the official star power at the grand opening of Hotel Liaison in just four weeks' time. She was happy to assume that role for her sister and also for what the hotel represented to her. It had become a refuge.

The employee, a stunning young woman named Ember, tore herself from the screen and grinned at her in welcome. Here, Kate was just Laurel's sister. She was even becoming friends with Laurel's partner, Stefanie Beresford. Having stayed with them when they temporarily lived in Seraphina Drake's Pacific Heights mansion, she marveled at what a pleasure it was to get to know the women who had brought Hotel Liaison back to life. She'd never really had a lot of female friends while growing up and was realizing how much she had missed.

Helping Laurel plan for the opening, she made calls to get sponsors and had met such interesting people. These women didn't look alike and talk incessantly about their next plastic surgery, who was or should be in rehab, their diet and exercise program, or even who was sleeping with whom. They actually had something to say. It was a refreshing break from her world in LA.

Just as she was about to hug Laurel she heard a familiar commotion on the street. It sounded like someone else had spotted her or others had spread the word that she was in town. She winked at Laurel and composed her face into her star persona, then turned to see another famous figure emerge from a limousine that had just arrived. She was assisted by Dasher Pate.

Greta Sarnoff was an up-and-coming and quite gorgeous young actress whose career was currently skyrocketing. She'd done a few independent films that, Kate grudgingly had to admit, revealed a lot of talent. She'd signed with Dasher Pate as her agent and her future seemed bright, including the Oscar buzz that Kate had yet to enjoy.

Whirling to meet Laurel's gaze, Kate demanded, "Is she staying here?"

"She who?"

"Dasher Pate, of course." Who else would she be talking about?

Laurel frowned slightly and held up a finger while she strode to another monitor and quickly checked a screen. "Yes. And Greta Sarnoff is the guest of Dasher Pate." She glanced up with a warm smile and seemed surprised to see that Kate was not happy.

"What?"

Kate felt her face heat and her hands rise to her hips. "Dasher Pate is staying here? For the beta-testing part? How did she get an invitation? And what is she doing with that *child*?"

"Well, I—"

"She got here by invitation and that child is twenty-three, not that it's any of your business." The husky alto behind her could belong to none other than Dasher Pate. Kate could never forget that voice.

Whirling to meet the warm gray eyes that accompanied it, the ones with the flashes of blue in them, Kate forced a smile. "Dasher, what a surprise. I had no idea you knew my sister. What a coincidence."

Dasher studied Kate in a way that made her skin prickle. She fought not to blush and cursed her fair complexion when her cheeks warmed. She knew blotchiness could not be far behind.

"Your sister? I haven't had that pleasure, but I've known Stefanie Beresford from the days when we worked for Beresford Hoteliers together. She invited me to help with the shakedown cruise of the hotel. Is there a problem?"

Laurel came to Kate's rescue by offering her hand to Dasher, introducing herself. "Stef mentioned that she'd invited a friend from her Beresford days. Thank you for coming and helping us out. I'm Laurel, Stef's partner, and Kate is my sister. She's on the volunteer crew, too. Kate will be our star attraction at our opening. Do you two know each other?"

"Not well," Kate quickly said. "We met five years ago." That's all that would come out so she closed her mouth and studied the front entrance, focusing on her breathing. Those yoga classes were handy for some things. She willed her blush away from her cheeks. Damn that Pate woman, it happened every time.

The silence grew, and Kate felt Dasher's eyes on her again. Finally, Dasher said, "I tried to get Kate to sign with me, but she decided Joe Alder would be better at guiding her career. Since then we've occasionally run into each other at premieres and award shows."

Dasher stood back and slowly took in the two of them. "You two definitely look like sisters. Both lovely." She was staring directly at Kate when she said "lovely," and her gaze lingered there for a moment before a noise toward the entrance of the hotel seemed to refocus her.

Sighing, she said, "Well, I've got to get back to Greta. The fans are probably at the overwhelm stage by this time. Plus, a couple of paparazzi in the group looked feral. Good to meet you, Laurel. Say hello to Stef for me and that I'll talk to her later. Good to see you, too, Kate."

She strode out to meet Greta, who was waving good-bye to the fans and signing a final autograph for the doorkeeper. Dasher was not extraordinarily tall, perhaps five foot eight, but her slim build and commanding presence made her seem taller. She laughed with Greta and casually slid an arm around her waist to guide her into the hotel and forestall a new wave of fans spotting her. The possessive gesture infuriated Kate.

She had to get out of sight. She grabbed Laurel, said "Show me your office," and practically hopped to the door next to the front desk, trying to relieve her ailing knee. Fiddling with her hair nervously while Laurel slid her ID card to get the lock to release, Kate made it inside with Laurel just as the front doors began to open.

"Care to tell me what that was all about?"

Laurel, as usual, was completely in the dark about appearances. "Laur, I couldn't be caught standing there like some admirer of Greta's. I'm a bigger name than she is. It would look terrible."

Laurel was silent for a moment. "Perhaps she's a fan of yours. Did you think of that?"

Kate snorted. "As in, 'I'm a big fan of yours, you has-been'? I think not. No, better not risk it." Zeroing in on a bank of monitors, she immediately found three different angles on the front desk. She watched as Dasher and Greta stood side by side and Dasher checked in. Both were smiling and laughing, seeming like friends. Or lovers.

"So you were avoiding Greta Sarnoff, not Dasher Pate. Correct?" Laurel, who was a shorter, slighter version of Kate but with the same unusual green eyes, had her arms folded across her chest and stood cocked on one hip. Kate was in no mood to discuss Dasher Pate.

"Dasher? Hell, no. I turned her down five years ago when we were both nobodies. Look what Joe Alder has done for my career. He made me a star, just like he promised."

"I thought you were bored with the roles you've been getting and tired of him controlling your every move. You even blamed him for insisting on you doing your own stunts in this movie. Dasher, from what I've read, has A-list actors and treats them really well. Maybe you should reconsider."

"You've read about Dasher? My sister reads about Hollywood? I'm shocked." Kate was trying to change the subject and hoped Laurel would get distracted.

Laurel grinned. "My sister, Kate Hoffman, is a big Hollywood celebrity, so of course I read about it. I can't go anywhere without seeing your face on a magazine cover or someone thinking I'm you, with smaller boobs. And don't forget the scheming we do when it's 'dump-time' for your boyfriends, or whatever you call them."

Kate had to admit that Laurel was always there for her. But the subject of Dasher Pate was not comfortable. That said, her sister was like a dog with a bone.

"So, what's the deal? Is she really a rotten person? Did she try to force you to her 'casting couch' or something awful?"

"No, nothing like that. She just...well, maybe I just feel bad. She's been nothing but professional with me. I didn't trust her to get me big jobs. Joe said that having a...a lesbian as an agent would almost certainly work against me in the film industry."

The words were out before she could edit them, and Kate didn't miss the hurt that registered in Laurel's expression. She hastened to add, "I'm sorry, sis, I'm embarrassed that I was ever that shallow. You know how much I love you and am happy for you and Stef. She's terrific. I was just so insecure and listened to every word that Joe said." This was all Dasher Pate's fault. She got Kate so distracted she blurted things before she thought about how she sounded.

"And now? She's very successful. What about now?"

With a huff, Kate said, "She's polite and cool. She'd probably laugh in my face and tell me what a no-talent actress I am. She'd follow that up with the thought that I can keep doing those inane romantic comedies and thrillers until I've had so much plastic surgery no one will recognize me."

"You haven't done any surgery, have you? You're beautiful just as you are. Don't go down that road, Kate."

"No, I haven't. Yet. Joe's making noises like I should, though. Why is it that in LA the male stars can look like shit into their nineties and they still have leading women in their twenties, while women are considered washed up at forty unless they've had major work done?"

"Because the men control most of the money and that's their fantasy. Every time I fly down to Los Angeles I'm astounded at the number of gorgeous women on the arms of these really ugly old guys with big grins. It's awful. Besides, you're only twenty-nine."

"Sis, let's not go there. It's hard enough." Until she uttered those words she hadn't realized how hard nearing thirty in the film industry really felt to her.

"Okay, sorry, Kate. I thought Dasher might be a respite

from that part of your career. She seems, I don't know, honorable."

Kate was surprised at her own tone when she ground out, "That opinion after meeting her for fifteen seconds. You did just watch her check in with that teenager, right? Being gay doesn't disqualify her from taking advantage of her position."

Staring at the monitors as Dasher and Greta walked toward the elevators, Laurel said, "Maybe, maybe not. I've always read that Greta was straight."

Kate huffed. "You know better than to believe what you read when it concerns Hollywood. Besides, I've known actresses who would bed anyone to get a role."

Staring at the smiling women on the monitor, Laurel said, "Well, Dasher Pate got separate rooms for them. So, draw your own conclusions."

CHAPTER TWO

Exhausted, Dasher dropped Greta off at her room and they promised to meet for dinner. She had a bunch of e-mails to answer and phone calls to make, and Greta was busy planning for her weekend in the wine country.

"Ah, youth." For some reason Dasher wasn't feeling particularly youthful these days. At thirty-two she was in good health and exercised faithfully, but she hadn't had fun in such a long time. She enjoyed Greta's exuberance, though, and had promised to whisk her away from the hectic merry-go-round her blooming career had set her on. If only for a weekend.

Greta had been restless lately, so Dasher decided it was better to bring her up here than for Greta to make a break for it. If that happened, who knew when she'd return? This way, Dash had more control. Sad, but true. Sometimes she hated this business.

Sighing, Dasher kicked her shoes off, then shrugged out of her suit jacket. She'd really rather be camping. Greta had invited her to indulge in the wine tasting, and she politely declined. If she'd begged her to go camping for a few nights, the temptation would have been hard to resist.

She'd spent time with her family in northern California as a kid. The air smelled different up here, particularly in the woods. In addition to the pine trees, the magnificent redwoods, eucalyptus, bay trees, all with their own distinctive odors, blended to make the air exhilarating. She'd played for hours with her imaginary friends and the forest creatures. Those were her fondest memories.

Having to stare at her computer burst that pleasant bubble. Running into Kate Hoffman hadn't helped. When Stefanie Beresford invited Dasher to the shakedown cruise of her new hotel, Stef said she wanted her to meet someone special. Stef told her she'd fallen in love and hadn't mentioned her love's name, only that she was a professor of some sort.

Even if Stef had said the name, Dash probably wouldn't have registered there could be a connection. Seeing Laurel and Kate together, Dash had no doubt. Those eyes. The sisters had large, lime green eyes surrounded by thick dark lashes that were mesmerizing.

They were certainly a major attraction for Kate's fans. Her eyes, her body, and her hair were all real. Dasher couldn't even let herself *think* of the drooling that went on about Kate's breasts. It made her want to stick a gigantic sweatshirt on her and hide her in a cabin in the woods.

Odd reaction over a woman who had dumped Dasher for a slimy agent and refused to be civil to her. Still, she hated it when others made derogatory or smarmy remarks about Kate Hoffman. She wouldn't put up with it for her own clients either. But Kate wasn't her client. And she was straight. She didn't need protection. Dasher had recited those reasons so often to herself they were beginning to sound like her mantra.

❖

After assuring herself that Dasher and Greta were staying on the lower floors, Kate picked up her Elysium card and limped to the private elevator toward the back of the lobby, obscured by a large potted plant. She swiped the card and held her hand to the scanning plate, and then the elevator door opened. As she stepped inside, a pleasant female voice greeted her by name. The lift smoothly rose to the top floor of the hotel and the voice gave her a weather forecast, wishing her a pleasant stay. A far cry from the first time Laurel had shown Kate around.

Then, only a year or so ago, they'd practically tripped over the holes in the musty hallway carpeting. They dodged construction debris and were expected to help out if someone needed a hand. On several occasions she'd even spent an hour or two schlepping buckets of this and that or holding one end of something until the other end was hammered or screwed into place. She'd enjoyed every minute.

Now, it all smelled new, but not overpowering. The hotel was finished with ecologically friendly paints, flooring materials, and fabrics. The windows in the rooms could open—not enough to toss oneself out of, but enough to capture a bit of the fresh cool sea breezes for which San Francisco was famous. She hated those hermetically sealed hotels she'd been forced to stay in when traveling on promotion junkets. She always ended up with a headache.

The heating and air-conditioning systems were completely filtered with monitors gauging particulate matter and automatic cleaning processes. They were wonderful for her allergies and similar to the ones at her home in Malibu. With each visit she found another reason this place was ideal for women travelers and for housing the Elysium Society.

The meeting of the society was the next day and she was looking forward to it. Never much of a joiner, she had been helping Laurel get things organized and had gotten to know many of the members. Irina Castic had a new project that she and Seraphina Drake had dreamt up, and they would be introducing it and calling for volunteers to staff it. They had been so secretive, and they literally giggled with each other when she and Laurel tried to wheedle information out of them. Her curiosity was piqued, to say the least. She and Laurel volunteered to be on that committee, no matter what it was.

Laurel had asked her and she surprised herself by saying yes. Being forced to sit with her leg up a lot of the time had given her not-always-welcome time to think about where she was in her life. The conclusion disheartened her.

Her career had taken up so much time, and she had few friends to show for it. Los Angeles and the fame business did not inspire trust or honor. She'd had many who claimed to be her friend, only to try to undercut her to get a role she was being offered or drop her if someone they thought better served them came along.

Last month Laurel sent her a refrigerator magnet. On it was a quote from Eleanor Roosevelt that said, "Do one thing every day that scares you." She laughed when she first read it. She had taken on Hollywood, she was a huge star. *That's scary stuff.*

All she really knew about Eleanor Roosevelt was that she had been a First Lady and she would never measure up to Hollywood standards of beauty. But curiosity sent her to the Internet to look her up. The woman would definitely have qualified as a member of the Elysium Society. When she mentioned her name to Seraphina and Irina, they wouldn't confirm or deny, but their eyes gave them away. They had met or known her, Kate was positive of that.

The quote stuck with Kate. What scared her? Perhaps friendship did. Her only true friend was Laurel. Her mind derailed to a stab of regret. Laurel had always been there for her, but Kate had blindly accepted that the woman Laurel was with before Stef was a good person, even though she personally didn't like her. She had ignored the obvious tension between them. The difference between that relationship and the one Laurel shared with Stefanie Beresford was night and day.

Seeing Laurel so happy made Kate wonder about exactly what had gone on with Laurel's ex. Laurel didn't talk about it, but Kate never pressed, either, a stance that was convenient for her. Only once had she dared to ask, and when Laurel gave her a tepid denial, she let it slide. She was so wrapped up in her own drama, she refused to see her sister shrinking away. To this day she wondered if Rochelle had been violent, but she was too cowardly to ask.

This new Laurel was a lovely, confident woman, and the contrast fascinated Kate. She must have been terribly brave to pull away from Rochelle's dominating personality.

The women who surrounded Laurel and Stefanie were wonderful and inclusive, but Kate still felt like an outsider. Probably because she'd always been an outsider. Oh, she was popular, the queen of this and that, but well liked? No one bothered to get to know anything more than what was on the surface. If she was really honest, she supposed she didn't try very hard in that department either. She didn't need to.

Friendships were formed by building trust, which took time and, yes, courage. Kate had read something like that recently and it struck her as true. She resolved then to follow Laurel's example and do one thing every day that scared her. If Laurel could do it, so could she. Hell, volunteering for that dumb committee, sight unseen, was scary. Of that she was sure. As the elevator doors opened to the Elysium floors, she felt better. She had a plan.

She let herself into her beautifully appointed suite. It had a large, comfortable working area with table and couch, and both the chair and desk were adjustable for height. Secure wireless ran throughout the building, with the Elysium floors having their own server, so she could plop anywhere with her laptop and check her e-mail without fear of being hacked or stalked. Oh, the joys of fame.

She kept cold wraps for her knee in the discreetly placed small refrigerator and was grateful for it and the fabulously stocked bar and wine selection in the common room. Members could help themselves or order whatever they wished. Now that she was off the pain meds she could explore what it had to offer.

The bed was luxurious, the bathroom shower had two showerheads and a steam vent, and the soaking tub that sat next to it had been suggested by one of the members of the society. The hotel's other special feature that appealed to Kate was its high level of security and privacy. She could look like hell, as if that was something she would even dream of doing, and not worry that someone would pull out their cell phone to grab a shot and later post it online. The Elysium Society members had a code of conduct that protected them all.

At the hotel Kate didn't have to worry about being followed to her room for an autograph or some guy deciding she was his next wife and wanting to prove it. She was getting more of those in Los Angeles, and Joe Alder was taking full advantage of such situations for the free publicity.

She had a huge argument with Joe on that subject just last week, even accusing him of hiring the stalkers to stir up the notoriety. He complained that if she would at least get arrested or have a public fight with someone, his job would be easier. She told him if he'd work harder to get her more challenging roles, her acting would do the talking for her. They'd become more contentious with each other over the past year, and she was just plain tired of it.

Joe had never been able to get her into bed, something he'd tried many times. Now he had a new actress who was more than willing to screw him, and if he could replace Kate with her, he would. He was even paying for her to get plastic surgery, making her look more like Kate each time. It was weird.

When Laurel had suggested that perhaps it was time to find a new agent, she had only voiced what Kate had been thinking about for some time, but was too insecure to act on. She'd made a mistake five years ago when she signed with Joe instead of Dasher.

She hadn't been thinking about only her career when she turned Dasher down. She was enormously attracted to her, a fact that had so many ramifications, it terrified her.

❖

Laurel poked her head into Stefanie's office and spotted her wearing her new glasses, staring at the computer screen. Laurel had insisted on the glasses when she caught Stef squinting and holding the papers far away to try to decipher them one too many times.

Stef resisted at first, saying she didn't want to give in to old age. When Laurel reminded her that she wore them and Stef had always responded passionately to them, Stef weakly pouted that it was only because Laurel looked incredibly sexy in them and she knew she wouldn't.

Plucking her own glasses off and putting them on Stef, Laurel dragged her to a mirror and made her look. Then she whispered something very naughty in her ear and told her how turned on she was because she looked terrific in them. Laurel chuckled at the memory, because the next morning Stef made an appointment with the ophthalmologist.

"Darling, are you busy?" She waited as Stef held up one finger, evidently hit Send, and swiveled to face her.

"Never too busy for you, Laur. What's up?"

"Not much, just missed you. Kate checked in, she's still limping a lot. But she seemed to forget about it when your friend Dasher Pate arrived with Greta Sarnoff. She almost carried me into the office to get away from them. That was after she and Pate had a tense but polite square-off. I didn't know they knew each other."

Stef removed her glasses and chewed on one stem, already familiar with ways to fiddle with them. "Wonder how they met. Dash and I've been buddies since my Beresford days. She tried hotel sales for a nanosecond, but discovered she's better at selling people than rooms. Did you meet her?"

Grabbing a quick kiss over the desk, Laurel settled into the chair across from Stefanie. "Yes, she's a knockout in a dark, brooding, alluring way, and seems very nice. Other than sparring with Kate, it all went smoothly. Strange, but Kate seemed miffed about *something*, I'm not sure what. She said she didn't want anyone to think she was admiring Sarnoff, but I swear seeing Dasher upset her. Very confusing."

Stefanie shook her head. "Well, if that upset her, wait until she finds out Dasher has been invited to join Elysium. She'll croak."

Laurel had forgotten that detail. "Should I warn her? The meeting's tomorrow."

Stefanie grinned at her. "Your sister has survived very nicely in the wilds of filmdom. I think she can handle this. Besides, maybe she'll get to know Dasher better and get over whatever this is. Dasher's truly one of the nicest, most loyal women I know."

Laurel nibbled her nail, not sure she wanted an answer to her question. "Were you two ever, you know, together?" She hated jealousy of any kind, but somehow she had to know.

"Lovers? No. That would be like sleeping with my sister. Ew. Now, sleeping with *your* sister…"

Laurel looked away and tried to hide her pain.

"Laur? What's wrong? I was only teasing…oh shit. I'm sorry, darling. That was thoughtless." She dropped her glasses and quickly rounded her desk and took Laurel in her arms and kissed her gently.

"I only have eyes and body and soul for you. I like Kate, but she's your sister and that's where it ends. Now, come on, let's go examine our new quarters in the executive suite. Surely we can find at least one surface we haven't made love on, if we look hard enough."

Stefanie held her close and seemed to wait for Laurel's reply. Her words about Kate had reminded Laurel of her former girlfriend Rochelle's obsession with Kate. But Stefanie's apology seemed heartfelt and made the memory of Rochelle's behavior fade more. Laurel relaxed in Stefanie's arms.

"We might be able to ferret out one or two. Sure you have time?"

Stefanie's deep brown eyes had turned almost black, and Laurel knew what that meant. "If we don't hurry I'm taking you right here, right now. I mean it."

"What about the elevator?"

"No. I don't want to entertain Security that much."

Grabbing Stefanie's hand, Laurel said, "Let's go."

❖

Across the street from the hotel, Chaz Hockaday and Michael Chiu snapped more exterior shots of the building while they waited for even more action.

"This is a goldmine!" Chaz said. "Not only do we have shots of Hoffman arriving but also Greta Sarnoff and Dasher Pate. The boss'll pay a load of money to see these. Then we can sell the ones he doesn't want. I told you taking this side job would pay off. Gimme five!"

Michael Chiu wasn't convinced. "Chaz, this still feels weird to me. We've got enough shots to pay the rent for a month, and I'm sure we'll get more. Why do we have to keep dogging these women at the hotel?"

Chaz shook his head. "Don't you get it? We're paparazzi, sometimes we don't eat. This dude is paying a freaking fortune for these shots. It's not personal, just business. Buck up, Mikey, my boy. We're in the cash now."

Michael sighed and propped himself against the building, the cameras that hung around his neck weighing him down. He was tired of watching the hotel, spying on Kate Hoffman, too. "How are we supposed to get into a 'women only' hotel? That door*woman* could play pro football. Did you see the stinkeye she gave us when we tried to follow Kate into the lobby?"

Chuckling, Chaz started removing cameras from his own neck and loading the equipment into their various bags and cases. "Nothing we haven't seen before. Besides, we'll figure out how to get in. Isn't it discrimination to allow only women?"

Michael admired Chaz's short curly brown hair, which framed unusually large blue eyes and perfect teeth. Not only was he handsome, but he could usually sweet-talk his way into most situations.

Michael couldn't wait to order a cosmo somewhere, so

he had begun to help Chaz with the equipment. "Not if it's a private club. I think they have some sort of membership thing happening. If it's by invitation only, we're screwed. We can't pass the physical."

"Well, maybe we'll let Mei-Lee do the work." Chaz gave Michael a suggestive look, and Michael knew he was focusing on his slight build and delicately beautiful Asian features.

"No way! If they found out I was in drag I could be in a bunch of trouble. Besides, Mei-Lee's very honest. She doesn't do this stuff. And she likes Kate Hoffman. Kate saved some of our friends' butts when they needed a beard to make them look straight. She's been nothing but supportive. I don't like this."

"Look, Hoffman's sister is with one of the owners of this place. Our job is to get a look at all of them and try to capture as many juicy shots of lesbians as we can. Frankly, we don't have a lot and we can't get inside. But with Hoffman being there so much, we may have found a way in. Besides, she and her sister look alike. Maybe we can doctor a photo to at least make people *think* she's gay. Or get a shot of her and her girlfriend making out. I only know the money's good."

Zipping the last case closed, Chaz stood and they started hurrying to the parking garage. "You don't have to like it. We'll just snag a few good shots. I wonder why Mr. Moneybags is so interested in trying to get something on Hoffman?"

"And why's he so interested in this hotel? Who cares if it's just for women?"

Chaz shook his head. "Probably because Hoffman comes here a lot. Well, we have enough for today. Let's drive over to the Castro. I do love to visit our home planet."

Michael sighed and hefted the duffel onto his shoulder while Chaz led the way toward the garage. How long would it take him to grow up and stop chasing the easy buck at the expense of others? More than that, what would it take to finally convince himself that following Chaz around and participating in these shady deals wasn't bringing them any closer? Chaz had only one man in his life: Chaz. Michael needed to stop dreaming that situation would change.

Chapter Three

Shades of gray blanketed the room and everything in it. Only the light from the windows made the machines and equipment in the workout facility visible. Dasher needed to do at least a light exercise routine, to counteract her sleeplessness of the night before. Besides, she preferred getting here before dawn so she could have the place to herself.

The night before, Stefanie gave her a tour of the gym with its impressive array of mats, mirrors, free weights, and machines. The tinted windows overlooked downtown San Francisco's Union Square, so the guests could enjoy the view without others watching them.

Tossing one of the soft white towels that were stacked in a row by the reception desk over her shoulder, Dasher walked to a section of mats where she could stretch and then quietly run through various forms of Tai Chi.

This type of exercise always relaxed and invigorated her at the same time. She usually did the routines on the beach behind her bungalow in Malibu, then ran for several miles. But she planned to forgo the run this morning because of the Elysium meeting at nine. She needed to work on the phone and computer for a few hours before the meeting. While normally she wore loose clothing for Tai Chi, today she had pulled on only a sports bra and workout tights, thinking she might try some of the other equipment.

After several minutes she became completely absorbed in the routines, her breath deepening with exercise, her blood humming with energy. She was vaguely aware that another early riser had entered the room, but since it was difficult to see, she assumed the other person either hadn't spotted her or was politely ignoring her.

By the time she focused on the facility again, the sun was seeping through the buildings and throwing light on some parts of the gym. She turned to pick up her towel and pack, then stopped.

The glow of the early morning bathed Kate Hoffman, who was running through what was obviously a well-learned yoga routine. Her blond hair was tied back but still reflected rays of gold. The simple workout tights emphasized her toned figure but didn't display it. She moved gracefully, fluidly. Dasher was spellbound.

She stood in the shadows, rooted to the mat. Kate was careful with her injured leg, taking time to stretch the knee gradually, breathing into the injury site, exhaling and allowing the probably tight muscles surrounding it to lengthen gradually. She was a vision.

She didn't seem able to flex the knee fully, but she was at an advanced level in all other aspects of her routine. She easily moved to a headstand and Dasher was to able pull herself from her reverie long enough to realize that she needed to leave, hopefully without Kate catching her gawking. She was certain that's how Kate would view her presence, even though Dasher was there first. Everyone else stared at her. Why would Dasher be different?

Silently moving toward the exit, she heard a squeak and

then a thud come from Kate's direction. When she whirled to see the problem Kate was hugging her knee, breathing rapidly. Dasher was instantly by her side.

"Kate! Are you okay?" She touched Kate, firmly grasped her upper arms, and made her look in her eyes. There she saw only pain and a weariness she'd never witnessed before. Without thinking she pulled Kate to her and rocked her gently, telling her it would pass, that she must have overdone it. Kate nestled into her arms, allowing the comfort.

The feeling of completeness lasted perhaps fifteen seconds before Kate stiffened and pushed Dasher away. "What are you doing? Spying on me? Get away." Her face was contorted in pain and anger, and perhaps a touch of embarrassment.

"Spying? No, no…I was exercising and then trying to leav—"

"Forget it, Pate. I saw you sneaking out. Can't I even have two minutes to myself to stretch? God!" She seemed to be warming up to a full tantrum.

"I wasn't *sneaking*, Kate. I was here first. I only noticed you when I was through and was trying not to disturb you. Geez, why does everything have to be about you?"

Kate stared at her, then huffed and scooted farther away. "It doesn't. It's just that you…startled me. I didn't know who you were and landed wrong when I came down too fast."

"I'm sorry. I really am. Is there anything I can do?" Dasher reached to help her up but Kate turned away.

Dash couldn't hold back the loud sigh of frustration that escaped her lips when she stood to leave. "Well, from now on I'll make a lot of noise if I see you before you see me. Have a better day." She left Kate on the mat, glaring after her.

❖

Kate waited until the door to the room clicked shut before she tentatively tried her knee. She'd have to put ice on it as soon as she got back in her room. She scolded herself for overreacting to Dasher's concern.

Truthfully, she'd come to the gym and instantly known it was Dasher across the room. Although she couldn't see her facial features clearly, the gradual dawn revealed her to be sinew and muscle beautifully folded onto a perfectly proportioned frame. Kate observed every muscle group, every nuance of motion, hypnotized by Dasher's grace and her quiet certainty.

When she was finally able to move to the farthest spot away from Dasher, she was unable to merely go through her yoga routines as best she could. She had to make them perfect, in case Dasher caught sight of her. She pushed too far, and when she fell from her headstand, the pain reminded her of the injury and how frightened she'd been at the time.

Then Dasher, damn her, had been there, and when Dasher held her, she made the pain bearable and the fear disappear. Of course Kate had to push her away and accuse her of being a rotten individual. She couldn't just accept Dasher's offer of compassion.

Sometimes she wondered about herself. What was it about Dasher Pate that didn't allow her to be friendly? Or even neutral? Every nerve ending, every emotion she possessed was uniquely tuned to that woman. She had schooled herself to be on guard for the intentions of most others, which were usually self-serving. On the rare occasions she was willing to admit it, hers certainly were.

But Dasher, for some reason, always got in under her defenses. Every damned time Kate had to consciously do—well—what she just did: Realize what she was doing and with whom she was doing it. She was accepting comfort from the enemy, that's what—comfort from someone who could have derailed her career before it even began, according to Joe Alder. Someone who could torpedo her even now.

It didn't matter that Dasher had never done anything overtly to hurt her. Or that she couldn't get Dasher's face out of her head sometimes. Or that when she was in Dasher's arms, being there felt the opposite of dangerous. It felt right. None of that mattered. All she saw was a big red warning sign.

She had to be constantly vigilant in order to head off any potential threats to her career, her image. However, she was tired and her image had begun to mean less to her, perhaps since her injury. Her defenses were probably just down because she'd overworked her knee. So naturally, when the pain hit, she was unable to push Dasher away before she... before she...allowed Dasher to care for her.

Kate limped to the common area that served as a meeting room for the society and found a comfortable chair with an ottoman on which to rest her now-swollen knee. She'd torn the medial meniscus and received a nice knock on the head while filming an escape scene in her latest thriller.

She chose a surgeon who would not only repair the knee and clean out all the other junk in there from years of athletics, but would leave barely a trace of a scar. As pretty as it was, it still hurt like hell and had only recently begun to feel better. Alder had pushed her to do some of her own stunts, and she willingly agreed. She was in good shape and figured she wouldn't have any problems.

She hadn't considered the time such stunts would require away from her actual acting responsibilities, or the athletic abilities needed. While physically she was capable, having to gut up to do the stunts took its toll and distracted her. She was now quite content to let the second-unit director and the stunt folks do their thing while she concentrated on her characters. No matter what Joe said, her fans *did* care if she could act, that rat bastard. She had the fan mail to prove it. Maybe most considered it a pleasant surprise, but she could act.

She looked around the tastefully furnished common area of the Elysium floors, which came complete with a beautiful young female attendant. Laurel said they employed a lot of college kids part-time, many that she had taught before she took her sabbatical. The young woman had brought her a pot of fresh Assam tea and a large cup that held more than two ounces.

Some of the members that Kate met at the first gathering of the Elysium Society began to arrive. They helped themselves to refreshments and found a spot to sit. Most waved or came by to say hello and reintroduce themselves, polite but not fawning. Kate was relieved and a bit disconcerted at the same time. She'd always been the center of attention, no matter where she went. Her physical beauty, and now her celebrity, almost guaranteed that.

As she looked around, she saw at least a half dozen women who could match her looks yet chose to avoid the limelight. She could practically tick them off on her fingers: a world-famous journalist who was Greek and beautiful, but seemed unaware of both her beauty and her status; senators; CEOs of large corporations. It was heady company—all looking fabulous but not preening. Kate decided she wanted to be that way. *Next meeting, less makeup, maybe no makeup.* The thought made her uneasy and she quickly shelved the idea.

She had to admit that she didn't have much experience in the world of not being the star. But she needed to learn.

Laurel did it so easily. Maybe she'd follow Laurel's example. A familiar voice brought her out of her reverie.

"Hey, Kate, how's the knee doing?" Stefanie Beresford settled gingerly on the ottoman, her warm chocolate brown eyes welcoming. Kate liked this woman more each time she saw her. She never uttered a smarmy double entendre like those Laurel's ex had constantly come up with. Stef seemed to be madly in love with Laurel, which Kate admired. She felt like she could trust her.

"It's better, but I like to elevate it when I can. Keeps any swelling down. I think I overdid it this morning in the workout facility. I'll give up the ottoman if someone needs it, though. How are you? I'll bet putting the finishing touches on the hotel has kept you busy."

Kate surprised herself by caring about Stef's reply, but then she attributed her interest to needing to know that the opening hadn't been pushed back, thereby screwing up her schedule. She rarely thought about anyone else's responsibilities.

Stef said, "It's been hectic, but Laurel has been a huge help. She's very organized, and she and Denny keep us all on track. To tell you the truth, I don't know what I'd do without her. On every level."

Stef's unabashed love for Laurel warmed Kate's heart, but she quickly looked away, uncertain why. Was she jealous? She really liked Stef and was glad for Laurel. But seeing her sister so happy made her own miserable love life stand out in glaring relief.

While she made the obligatory rounds of parties and award shows, for the most part, that's all they were: a to-do list. The public-relations machine constantly ground out rumor and innuendo about her being seen with her latest leading man, at least until the opening of the film, which was when they usually quietly parted ways. She'd always told herself this was simply the way the business was, but lately she'd begun to understand the toll that kind of lying and distortion could take on an individual.

She'd watched talented actors and actresses succumb to the drugs and alcohol that those who wished to control them so willingly provided. She'd seen women with their own distinct look submit to being cut and dyed, waxed and Botoxed into someone else's vision of beauty. She wondered what price she would eventually be willing to pay. At the very least, she seemed willing to sacrifice the type of love Stefanie and Laurel enjoyed.

Stefanie's voice broke up her pity party. "Kate? Hello?"

"Um, sorry, Stef. What were you saying?" She was surprised to see the concerned expression on Stef's face.

"I wanted to tell you about a new member before she's introduced. Laurel said you might want to know."

Kate's attention was drawn to the smiling woman behind Stef. Dasher Pate. Gray eyes, ringed with thick eyelashes, held hers for the second time that morning and wouldn't let go.

Stef's voice intruded. "Kate? What are you…oh." Stef had followed Kate's line of sight. Quickly standing, she gave Dasher a hug.

"Hey there, welcome. I gather you two have met." Stef stood aside with a hopeful expression.

Kate didn't intend to embarrass anyone by causing a scene, so she stayed where she was but offered her hand to Dasher. "Hello, again. Are you joining the Elysium Society?"

Dasher's warm touch sent a current to every part of Kate's body and she jerked her hand back. Alarmed and confused, she felt her cheeks begin to burn immediately. *Damnit*. She should have remembered that about Dasher. Never touch.

Kate could swear Dasher was smirking as she casually

said, "I'm thinking about it. Does it mean I get to stay on these floors? I thought the lower floors were wonderful, but these are spectacular." She looked around and waved to a few women she evidently knew.

Still flustered, Kate snapped, "It has a lot more to it than plush accommodations, so if that's your only interest, stay at the Four Seasons."

Dasher's smile disappeared and her jaw muscles worked, but she didn't speak. After a moment she quietly said, "Stef, talk to you later," then walked to the other side of the room and found a chair. Several others quickly engaged her in conversation.

Stef hesitated, then said, "Kate, I didn't know you disliked Dasher so much. Do you want me to ask her to leave?"

"What? No, of course not. I must be irritable because of my knee. It aches terribly today. We just seem to clash. I'm sure Dasher would be an asset to the society. Sorry, Stef."

Giving her a relieved and likely grateful grin, Stef moved quickly off to greet others.

Kate surprised herself with her apology and suspected she owed one to Dasher, too. This whole weekend was turning out to be an emotional roller coaster for her, and that had not been the plan.

Damn that Dasher Pate anyway. This happened every time she ran into her and was a big reason she avoided her when possible, or at least tried to anticipate running into her. She needed to be prepared. She'd been blindsided just now, which was why she'd reacted so poorly. Working a confusing situation like this out in her head always made her feel better.

The room was completely full and buzzing in anticipation. Laurel had taken Stef's vacated spot on the ottoman and patted Kate's leg reassuringly, her attention on Irina Castic and Seraphina Drake.

The Elysium Society had been recently reborn, primarily because of Irina and Seraphina's efforts to keep its flame alive through some hard times. Also, the tenacity of Stefanie Beresford to rehabilitate the hotel and the curiosity of Laurel, who kept digging into the hotel's past, had made this new beginning possible.

In order to secure not only the future of Hotel Liaison, but that of the Elysium Society as well, Irina had used a portion of the funds generated from selling land recently restored to her family in Serbia. Now the society would always have a home and no one could usurp it. Few knew the whole story of its rebirth, but all present waited to find out the next phase of the society.

Seraphina used a fork to tap her cup lightly, and the room quieted. She smiled at the gathering of women who had pledged to make the world a safer place in which to live. For that was their charge: all issues that related to the status of women. The difference between their organization and others was the fact that, except for the façade they were creating, its work was secret, and sometimes it might involve risk.

Her voice was commanding and easy to hear. "We welcome you to this meeting. We have been diligently working on reestablishing the structure of the Elysium Society while the hotel has been nearing completion. You see before you our dream come true."

The appreciative hum produced a smile on Laurel's and Stef's faces, and Kate's, too. She knew how many eighteen-hour days Laurel and Stef had put into the project. It certainly appeared worth it. This hotel was perfect for women, and it wouldn't take long for word to get around. Stef had told her that if all went well, it could be self-sustaining within two years.

Seraphina continued. "Each of you filled out an extensive

questionnaire about your skills, interests, training, and connections. Our committees and projects will need your expertise, and we will take advantage of it. Some of the projects will provide new experiences for you, and you will learn a great deal about yourselves as you tackle them. Everyone has the right to turn them down, but please consider carefully before you do."

She turned to Irina Castic, who was sitting to her left. Seraphina was tall and robust, and Irina was her opposite. She was small, with delicate bones, her face exquisitely structured. Kate would have cast her as royalty without a second thought. She smiled at the thought because, as it turned out, Irina *was* royalty. She'd had a difficult life but now she was reunited with Seraphina, and they would spend their remaining years together. She looked radiant.

Kate's eyes welled up, and she pulled her thoughts back to the meeting, chastising herself for being such a complete romantic. She glanced away from Irina and caught Dasher's concerned gaze. Confused for a second, she realized that Dasher had seen her tears and thought something was wrong.

Reflexively she grinned and gave an embarrassed shake of her head, looking back at Irina as she started to speak. She didn't hear a word, though. Her thoughts centered on the expression on Dasher's face. She seemed genuinely worried. Kate couldn't remember anyone but Laurel bothering to notice her sad moments, except perhaps to tell her to dial it up or down, depending on the scene. But she did recall that fact about her brief meetings with Dasher five years before and, recently, at the gym. Dasher cared. Did Dasher treat all women with such tenderness?

Seraphina had finished her presentation, and Irina was talking about the projects Elysium was thinking of taking on. "The first, and probably the most public, will be the Elysium

Foundation. We will be awarding grants to projects that promote women: our history, our dreams, our concerns. We will also give educational grants to individuals who show high potential and a desire to help others learn. We'll need volunteers to help guide this committee and make selections."

Several hands shot up and Irina looked at Laurel, who held up a clipboard and said, "I'll pass around the sign-up sheets after Irina is through."

Irina continued. "We have several initial grants to announce. First, a full scholarship to the university of her choice, to Miss Ember Jones. Ember was my roommate for a bit and has worked very hard to build this hotel. Ember, please stand."

Ember rose—tall, blond, and lovely, blushing deeply, seemingly embarrassed at the attention. Kate had seen her around the hotel, mostly in the company of Irina and Seraphina, and also assisting the designer of the interior of the hotel. Yesterday she'd been at the front desk when Kate checked in. Kate thought she was Irina's grandchild, but Laurel said they weren't related.

The group applauded and Kate noticed that Jock Reynolds, the general contractor for the renovation of the hotel, and Denny Phelps, Stef's business partner, gave Ember a whistle and applauded louder than the rest. Ember sat down quickly and they gave her a few high fives.

"Next, a full scholarship to the law school of her choice, we're hoping Hastings or Stanford Law to keep her close, to Agnes Brady, without whom Hotel Liaison might not be here, and I would not have been reunited with my Seraphina. Although several men promised to block her acceptance no matter where she applied, the deans who are members of this society will make sure she's welcomed with open arms." A big round of applause sounded for Agnes, the loudest by a tall lanky woman named Lefty Lebowski, Agnes's love. Kate still wasn't sure if Lefty talked. All she did around Kate was blush and trip over things. Kate had a lot of fans, male and female, who behaved the same way, and she always found it endearing.

After the list was completed a few moments later, it took a minute for everyone to settle down again. Kate peeked at Dasher, only to find her chatting with Ember, probably congratulating her on her scholarship. Or hitting on her. Cynicism was alive and well in Kate's world.

"Now, last on our list, for the moment, is a pet project that we have long thought of but never considered possible. I have memories of starvation and hardship when I was young and World War Two was raging. Often, women were last, if we were lucky enough to have the government even consider us. We were there to service the men and children. Men because we were told to, children because we wanted to."

Kate could feel the anticipation in the room. "We want to find and establish a property outside the city. We want it to be self-sustaining, 'off the grid,' as my younger friends say. A location to which women can turn should times be hard for us. It will be connected to others that will be established in the future."

Kate was amazed at the constant innovation of these women. She'd never thought of something like that.

Irina followed by saying, "We need a committee to search for locations." With a sweet smile, she continued. "Several have already volunteered to be on it, no matter what, and we thank them. Any of you who have suggestions for locations, please provide them. And we need a few more volunteers. You don't need any experience in real estate, but some familiarity with farming or camping would help. We'll have experts to advise us once we've secured the location."

A sinking feeling in Kate's gut told her she was among the no-matter-what volunteers, and the glimmer in Laurel's eye confirmed her suspicion. *Oh, no.* She definitely wasn't an outdoorsy kind of woman. No room service was her idea of roughing it. She immediately began to dream up excuses. *Oh dear, my schedule is too booked. Oh gosh, my knee is killing me. I have to fly to Spain for a shoot just when we'd be going on the trip. When did you say it was?*

Realizing that she'd committed herself and seeing the huge grin on Laurel's face, she knew she'd just have to hope for some five-star hotels nearby wherever they searched. She *knew* there was a reason she never volunteered.

Laurel stood and announced, "When the clipboard reaches you, please sign under the committee that strikes your interest. If none appeal, suggest something that does and we'll tap you eventually, don't worry." The appreciative laughter told Kate that all there were willing when the time came.

Watching Laurel shake hands and exchange hugs as she worked her way toward her, Kate felt a slight uneasiness when Dasher asked for the clipboard and wrote her name on one of the committees. She was busy talking to that Stryker woman and her gorgeous partner, so didn't seem to pay too much attention to the page itself.

Reasoning that Dasher probably signed up for the scholarship committee, she took a few breaths to calm down. No way would that woman want to get dirty schlepping around the woods. Her suits were hand tailored and the short nails on her strong hands manicured perfectly. She probably felt the same way Kate did, except Kate had boxed herself in. Wouldn't you know?

❖

That night Kate had dinner with Stef, Laurel, Denny, and Jock in the newly refurbished gourmet café run by Sika Phelps, Denny's mother. Jock had chosen the perfect wine, and they were all feeling mellow by the time the late-harvest Zinfandel was served after dessert. Kate was resting her knee on a chair next to her and feeling less pain than usual.

Denny asked, "Say, who's on that new search committee? I want to be, but I'm sure I'll be here until after we open the hotel. Jock?"

Holding up both hands, Jock said, "Don't look at me. I'd be shot if I deserted the troops this close to completion. And, Stef? Don't even think about going anywhere or I'll chain you to your desk and only trot you out when the building inspectors show up. I don't think Laurel would like that."

Stef grinned, and Kate noticed how red her blush was. She guessed that the lovebirds were as busy at night and early in the morning with each other as they were all day with the hotel. She chose to ignore her flash of envy.

"Yeah, maybe once the site is secured, I can help. Laur, you could take a weekend if you wanted."

Stef's voice had a faint whine, which told Kate that she would truly miss Laurel. But Kate appreciated Stef's willingness to let her and Laurel spend some time together. They seemed to get closer each time Kate visited, and Kate had begun to enjoy their growing intimacy more than she ever thought she would.

Laurel gave Stef a loving look, as if she knew how much Stef would miss her. Shit, Kate thought. It was obvious that Laurel would rather stay here with Stef than leave town with the committee. Maybe if Laurel bowed out, Kate could do so too, though she'd hate to disappoint Laurel after she'd spent so much time and energy persuading Kate to volunteer for the committee.

"Hon, we promised," Laurel said. "Maybe we can push back the date to after the opening, but we both need to help. Besides, Kate would be crushed, right, Kate?"

Mustering up her best smile, Kate gritted her teeth and said, "Right, sis. Devastated."

From the sound of things, Kate would be doing the site surveys by herself. Oh, well, maybe it wouldn't be so bad after all. Now if Dasher and that Greta woman would just finish their meal and leave the café, she could relax and not have to concentrate so hard to avoid looking in their direction.

As it was, she knew each course they'd eaten and had missed most of the conversations at her own table because she was trying so hard to hear what Greta and Dasher were talking about. They seemed very relaxed, like friends.

Kate couldn't help but compare their apparent ease with each other with her own relationship with Joe Alder. She had to force herself to be civil to the man. When she woke up in the hospital after her injury she vividly recalled him screaming at some poor nurse and then firing one of her bodyguards for apparently allowing a fan into her room. He was such an ass.

Finally, much to Kate's relief, Dasher and Greta left, waving to their table as they exited the dining room. Greta was a beauty, in a very distinctive way. Kate was sure Dasher didn't pressure her into constant cosmetic surgery to make her look like everyone else.

She forced her attention away from Dasher and Greta and back to the table. Stefanie was saying, "Okay, the photo shoot is scheduled for eight thirty. Kate, if you could be down by eight for makeup, we can wrap it pretty quickly. Is that okay?"

"Hmm? Oh, yes, of course. Not a problem." It certainly wouldn't be a problem, since Kate would be avoiding the workout facility like the proverbial plague.

Chapter Four

Dasher stared at the ceiling the next morning as the light in her room gradually grew brighter. She'd been awake for a while but couldn't dredge up enough energy to get out of bed. Maybe if she'd pulled the blackout drapes closed she would have gotten some sleep.

What a stupid mistake to eat dinner in the hotel last night. What was she thinking?

Greta had talked her into it because she'd heard good things and wanted to try it out. Even though Greta's own fame was on the rise, all the famous women she'd seen arriving for the meeting had left her a bit starstruck. She admired Kate Hoffman a lot, but Kate refused to be more than polite, and only to Greta. She ignored Dasher completely.

Dash hated to admit it, but that bugged her. After five years she should be immune to Kate's rudeness, but she wasn't. So what? Wasn't that just business as usual in Hollywood? She had thought Kate was someone who cared, but she turned out to be just like most of the other shallow, self-serving…damn.

That wasn't true. Most folks in her industry were hardworking, wonderful people, with some dramatic exceptions. The truth was, five years ago Dasher had fallen for Kate Hoffman. From the moment they met, and no matter how hard Dasher tried, no one else could measure up to Kate. For a few blinks Dasher convinced herself that Kate returned the feeling. What a fool she'd been. And yesterday morning—

A knock on the door pulled her back to the room and told her it was time to get on with the day and save the recriminations for another sleepless night. Tossing on some sweats and noting how quickly room service had arrived, she opened the door to see Stefanie, smiling at her with big doe eyes.

"Stef?" She looked behind her and saw a small service table. "Are you doubling as the delivery person? Wow, this *is* personal attention."

Still grinning, Stefanie hopped around to push the table into the room. "No, your order will be up soon. I just thought we could have coffee together and chat a bit. Haven't seen you in so long, you know?" She set up the coffee service, complete with a French-press carafe, on the table in front of the couch. She was fussing a lot.

"Stefanie. I've never known you to wait on anyone. Or be nervous. Is something wrong?"

Stefanie straightened abruptly, blushing. "I, ah, have a favor to ask."

Without thinking, Dasher said, "Sure. Anything for you." When the words were out of her mouth, she realized that normally that would be true, but with Kate Hoffman on the premises...*uh-oh.* Stef wasn't blind. She'd probably noticed the tension between them.

With some trepidation she asked, "What do you need?"

Stefanie blurted without preamble, "We have a photo shoot this morning using Kate and my brother for the advertising to promote the opening of the hotel and the other model was a no-show and we can't replace her and you're the only one that could fit into the clothes and look decent and you're just what we need and I hate to ask but we really are desperate and we're paying a fortune for the whole setup and..." Finally she paused to gasp for air and Dasher held up her hand.

"Me? Model? I don't have experience and would feel stupid in a dress. Have Laurel do it. They'd look great together."

"We're planning to take some photos of them. It's another shot we're looking for."

"Then Greta. Wait, she's probably already left with her friends. Why me?" Dasher was feeling a bit panicky.

"Well, the clothes. They'd fit you perfectly. And...and..." Stef was now addressing the coffee cups, hands behind her back.

"And what?" Dash was quiet. She'd seen the look before and knew Stef was deciding how to spin this.

"We need someone who isn't all frilly, you know? Someone darker to contrast with Kate's blondeness. Someone who will appeal to a broader range of women. Someone—"

"Butch."

"Laurel used the word 'androgynous' and I thought of you." Judging from the expression on her face, Stefanie was trying to sell this as a plus, and when Dasher thought about it, she couldn't argue. She had never been a classically feminine child or woman. Wearing a dress ranked below picking up a dead rat with her bare hands on her queas-o-meter, and she wasn't much on wearing makeup. She almost nodded until she remembered with whom she'd be spending time.

"You want me to be in a photo shoot with Kate Hoffman. Who evidently hates my guts. Does she know about this?"

From Stef's refusal to meet her eyes, she guessed the answer was no. Dasher's jaw muscles tightened, something that was becoming a habit around Kate Hoffman. "When did you intend to tell her?"

The air went out of Stefanie, and she drooped into the chair next to the couch. "We just found out. We thought we'd get your agreement, and then when you showed up it would be too late for Kate to pitch a diva-fit in front of the photographer and my brother Jason. Laurel swears Kate wouldn't do that, but I don't know her. She might."

Stef got to her feet and shuffled to the door. She looked so pitiful Dasher couldn't help herself. "Wait. I'll do it. What the hell, it's only for an hour or so, right? I can endure Kate Hoffman for that long." More accurately, the question was probably how long Kate could endure Dasher.

The transformation in Stefanie gave her whiplash. "Really? Thanks! This is great." She flew to the food cart and suddenly produced several hangers' worth of clothes covered with a zipped bag sporting a designer label and tossed it on the couch.

Flinging open the door, she said, "Enjoy your breakfast, on the house, of course, and be down for makeup in an hour." With that, she was gone. It wasn't even seven a.m.

Dasher stood there, trying to figure out what had just happened. More importantly, she was trying to figure out why she wasn't angry. Judging from the drunk moths fluttering in her stomach, she was excited.

She watched the city wake up outside her window as she sipped her coffee, deep in thought.

❖

The bustle in the lounge portion of the hotel lobby had drawn a small crowd of onlookers. Lights, cameras, and furniture were being rearranged, and power cords were run and taped down to keep anyone from tripping.

Laurel and Stefanie stood to the side, Laurel nervously shifting from one foot to the other while Stefanie repeatedly glanced first at her watch, then toward the elevators.

"Don't worry," Stef said. "Dasher will show. I wonder where everyone is? The makeup person arrived ten minutes ago."

Behind her, a deep male voice crooned, "Is this the place where I become famous?"

Both of them wheeled around to see the smiling face of Jason Beresford, Stef's younger brother. He wore jeans and a white button-down shirt and had a bag of clothes on hangers slung over his shoulder.

Laurel hugged him. "At least we have our leading man. We can get you into makeup and wardrobe while we wait for the others."

"Oh, makeup. Well, why not? This shoot should make me the hottest bachelor in town. I might even have to move here."

Laurel watched as Stef took her brother by the arm and aimed him toward the crew that was assembling the shoot. He was a few inches under six feet, with an athletic build and the same chestnut hair and soft brown eyes that always made Laurel need an extra breath when Stefanie entered a room.

Stefanie's older brother, George, hadn't spoken to her since she foiled his plan to steal the hotel from her. Somehow it was all Steffi's fault. Laurel and Stef were happy to have him neutralized—neutered was how Laurel liked to think of it.

In contrast to George, Jason had stood by Stef the whole time and they'd grown closer because of his support. He readily agreed to the photo shoot so he could brag to his friends about being in the same room with Kate Hoffman.

Jason had turned out to be a pleasant surprise for Laurel. Her own brother was, well, self-involved. Ted pretty much did what he wanted, when he wanted. As the only boy, he was the chosen one. When Kate was born, he was jealous for a while, then just ignored them both and went on his way, involving their parents in his life as he saw fit. Holidays with the family were polite, mostly filled with stories of her brother and Kate. Laurel had to smile. Actually, since she and Stef had found each other, suddenly Laurel wasn't just the family bookworm anymore.

As if conjured up, someone elbowed to the front of the crowd in the lounge, creating a slight disturbance. Suddenly a familiar woman was waving happily at Laurel.

"Oh, my God," Laurel said.

Marilyn Hoffman started toward her but their security woman stopped her. She looked bewildered until Laurel signaled it was okay for her to join them. Marilyn hustled over and gave Laurel a quick hug, then looked around for a place to put her small suitcase.

"Mom, what are you doing here?" Laurel desperately tried to find Stef to warn her. Kate was going to have a fit.

"Both of my daughters are together in one place and I wanted to see how things are going, of course. Now, where is Kate and where is Stefanie?" Marilyn was busily scanning the shoot site, then started waving madly at Stef, who almost tripped over an electrical cord when she saw her.

After only a second, she seemed to recover and plastered a smile on her face. "Marilyn! What a surprise." She glanced meaningfully at Laurel, who could only try to convey her own mystification with a slight shrug.

Her mother was peppering Stef with questions about the hotel when Laurel noticed the elevator doors opening. Dasher exited and strode toward them, mouth set in a straight line. Under her breath, Laurel whispered, "She looks hot."

Clad in soft, form-hugging chocolate leather from head to toe, Dash wore only a skimpy camisole under her jacket, and it hinted at her breasts. It was better than a cat suit. She looked dangerous.

Stef had almost reached Laurel and Mrs. Hoffman when she spotted Dasher. She halted and said, "Whoa."

Suddenly Dasher was standing in front of them. "I feel like an idiot," she said, and Laurel elbowed Stef to bring her around. Her mother had fallen silent and stared.

Laurel tried to get things moving by saying, "You look terrific, Dasher. You should think about buying that outfit. It looks like it was made for you."

"It sure does," Marilyn commented.

Glancing in obvious confusion at the new woman, Dasher said, "Do I know you? You look familiar."

Not missing a beat, Mrs. Hoffman said, "Why, I'm the mother of the Hoffman girls. Don't you see the resemblance?" She smiled expectantly.

Laurel thought Dasher's smile was automatic when she said, "Of course, all beautiful."

While Marilyn cooed, Dasher turned to Laurel. Tapping her camisole, she said, "I couldn't wear a bra under this. It's, like, see-through or something. Who the hell wears stuff like this outside of LA? I can't take the jacket off, so don't even ask."

"Well, I—"

"Dash, you look amazing." Stefanie finally recovered. "Doesn't she, Marilyn?"

"Why, yes, in a very, um, handsome way."

"Yeah, amazingly stupid." Dasher was a bright pink and wouldn't look at them. She stood with her arms folded tightly across her chest.

Laurel turned her and pushed her toward the area where the studio artist had almost finished applying Jason's makeup. "Don't worry, Dasher. This will all be over soon and we're *so* grateful. You know Stefanie's brother Jason, right?"

Jason pulled the towel from around his collar and stood with a grin, extending his hand. "Dasher? Good to see you.

I was in college when you and Stef hung out. Are you my competition today?"

As they shook hands, Dasher said, "Of course I remember you, Jason. We teased you unmercifully. Competition?" She gave Laurel a questioning look.

Before Laurel could reply Jason said, "Yeah, for the favors of the beautiful Kate. That's kind of the theme for the shoot. Didn't Stef tell you?"

Just then Kate arrived, which caused all the onlookers to direct their attention toward her. Already clad in a diaphanous ball gown, makeup evidently in place, she stopped to sign a few autographs, and when she turned her attention to the scene, her eyes locked immediately onto Dasher's.

Laurel was frantically trying to think of something to say to warn Kate about their mother and head off an embarrassing confrontation, but stopped. Kate's expression was one of surprise, but also something else, something Laurel had never seen in her, at least not since stardom. For a wisp of time she could swear she detected longing, maybe even tenderness. And when Kate's eyes swept up and down Dasher's body, could that have been lust? Then the curtain fell and her beautiful features hardened into a mask of anger.

Marching over to their small group, and without looking at Dasher, Kate demanded, "What is *she* doing here?"

Laurel calmly said, "Who? Dasher or Mother?" That stopped her.

Stefanie appeared, dragging Marilyn Hoffman with her, and quickly injected, "Kate, thanks for being kind of on time. Look at all these fans, just ogling and listening and dying to call the tabloids. That might be good for you, but not for us. And your mom surprised us. Okay?" She gave her a pleading look and Kate seemed completely confused.

Laurel said, "Why don't we clear the lobby and put up the screens. Then we can get this shoot under way." She had gently turned Kate away from Dasher so she was facing her and their mother.

Instantly, Kate said, "Mom, what a surprise. Laurel? Good idea. I have a few…questions." She glanced meaningfully at Dasher, then flounced over to the makeup chair that Jason had just vacated and dropped into it. "I shouldn't take long, just a touch-up. Dasher won't mind." Her green eyes flashed evilly at Dasher, who seemed stunned into silence.

Turning her attention to Jason, whom Kate had met the last time she was in San Francisco, she said, "Jason, my leading man. Good to see you." She fairly oozed sexy at him. Jason immediately rewarded her with a blush and some babbling, and her mother looked thrilled.

Laurel observed Dasher's unhealthy color and guided her away from the scene, then directed some of the staff to clear the lounge area of people. She never released Dasher's arm.

"Why does she always do that? Why does she talk as if I'm not even in the room?" The frustration and hurt in Dasher's voice pulled at Laurel.

"Dash, look at me."

Seeming to have to tear her eyes away from Kate, Dasher met her gaze.

"Would you say that Kate is a good actress?"

Huffing, Dasher answered, "Of course. Better than anyone knows, thanks to that skank of an agent."

Shoving that piece of information to the back of her mind, Laurel said, "Well, then, you should know when she's acting. I do. Especially because Mother just popped up."

She left Dasher standing by herself as she walked over to talk Kate down.

❖

Twenty minutes later Kate and the photographer, Susan Yang, were in full swing, and Dasher was eyeing them from the chair when the makeup artist would allow it.

"She's something, isn't she?" The woman was expertly applying base and shadow to Dasher's eyes. "I've done her makeup for two movies and she's a dream to work with. So nice."

Leaning back, Dasher glumly replied, "I wouldn't know."

The artist ignored her comment. "Wow, you have huge eyes and thick, dark lashes. I'll bet you don't need to wear much makeup."

"No." She was still trying to puzzle out Laurel's remark.

"Okay, close 'em." When Dasher next opened her eyes, the scene before her featured Kate in Jason's arms, both smiling at the camera. He was dressed in a beautifully tailored business suit and she was still in the gown. Stealing a glance at Mrs. Hoffman, she could almost see the woman imagining Kate in a bridal dress.

The photographer took quite a few photos, with assistants changing the lighting, switching cameras when she needed a different one, and scurrying around to fix details in the composition.

Finally, Susan called Dasher over and began to explain the next shots to her. While she talked, a beefy guy walked a huge Harley Davidson VRSC V-Rod Muscle motorcycle onto the set and set the stand. He and another man also hefted a large fan into position in front of the Harley.

"First, I need you and Jason on either side of Kate. We'll do takes of Jason and Kate, his arm around her waist while you, wearing wraparound sunglasses, will fold your arms and turn toward the bike. No smiles from you." Dasher nodded, desperately wanting to not screw this up and make a fool of herself. At least the no-smiles part would be easy.

"Next, we'll have Kate kind of hang on your shoulder and stand all flirty." Kate and Dasher simultaneously said, "Flirty?"

Oblivious, the photographer continued. "No shades on this one. You're still facing away but looking over your shoulder, like, dubiously. Jason will act surprised, then maybe a bit pissed." Dasher and Kate merely stared at each other while they listened, Dasher in disbelief at what she was hearing and Kate for probably the same reason. Jason seemed absorbed in what expression to use to look "pissed" because his face was pretty animated.

"And last, Dasher, you'll be on the bike, the fan will be blowing, Kate will be behind you with her arms around your waist, and you two will smile at each other. It's another shot of you looking over your shoulder, but this time, you both are really enjoying it." The entire time she kept clicking the damned camera.

Kate said, "Do I have to hug her? Maybe I can just lean back and look like I'm loving the motorcycle ride. I'll give you a huge smile." She demonstrated for Susan.

"Nah, we want there to be a hint of intrigue here. Besides, you'd fall off the bike."

That did it for Dasher. "What's wrong, Hoffman? Too homophobic to chance touching the big bad dyke?" Off to the side she heard someone gasp and assumed it was Mrs. Hoffman.

Kate's eyes enlarged and then narrowed dangerously. "Nonsense. I was just… Never mind, you wouldn't understand the creative process anyway."

Dasher bristled at the slight, but held her tongue. "Let's just do this."

Susan was directing her crew and ignored them. Jason was probably being polite because he was preoccupied with his nails.

It went as well as it could with Dasher trying not to grind her teeth and Kate overtly flirting with Jason. When they added a shot with the three of them facing the camera and glancing at each other sideways, they did all dissolve into laughter, Jason leading the way. That blew off some of the tension.

As they were positioning themselves for the final Harley shot, Dasher was about to mount the bike when she saw Kate stumble and begin to fall. She'd noticed her limping slightly earlier but didn't want to risk another insult by showing concern.

Dasher jumped away from the bike and was able to catch Kate under her arms to prevent her from hitting the floor. As she lifted her carefully to her feet, Kate stared at the soft leather she was clutching, then at the cleavage the camisole wasn't hiding, and then their eyes met. Kate didn't pull away but after a moment seemed to remember where she was, and who she was. She blushed a pretty pink and stared at Dasher's hands on her. Dasher let go.

"Thanks. Darned knee."

"Maybe some ice." *Lame, lame, lame*.

Susan interrupted. "Okay, let's do this shot and then one more, same thing, but Kate will be in jeans and a tank top. Dasher, for that you'll fully unzip the jacket. Let's go."

Touching Kate had made Dasher hyperaware, hypersensitive to her presence. When Kate slid her arms around Dasher's waist, and they were directed to look at each other and smile, she must have looked like a love-struck kid instead of a tough biker, because Susan just kept shooting.

Then, she had to wait an excruciating amount of time

while Kate changed into jeans, a tank the color of her eyes, and big biker boots. She looked gorgeous.

Susan Yang said, "Great. Now, Kate, scooch in closer to Dasher and squeeze your arms around her waist while Dasher, you look over your shoulder at her." To the technicians she said, "I want that fan blowing on high, mostly on Kate."

At least Dasher got to put her shades on for that one. Instead of the kleig lights, the body contact with Kate was making her sweat and have to work hard to control her breathing. She hoped the freaking camera didn't pick up her practically nude breasts, which were now on point, under the jacket. She did get the maniacal smile right. She was almost nuts by the time Diana called it a wrap.

Kate seemed exhausted, too. She only mumbled and limped toward the elevators, her mother bustling after her.

❖

An hour later the last of the photo equipment was finally out of the area, and Laurel and Stef were putting the furniture back in place.

Stef said, "Well, that went okay, considering."

"Yeah." Laurel was straightening runners on sideboards, replacing lamps, candles, flowers, and letting Stef do the talking.

"I mean, they could have killed each other, or Kate could have refused to work with Dash. So, it went well, right?"

"Um-hmm." So far, Laurel had yet to look at her.

Stopping mid shove of a large leather chair, Stef said, "Is there something you aren't saying? I'm not used to one-word answers."

Laurel turned to Stefanie. "Did you notice anything about

the two of them? I mean when they weren't avoiding each other."

Staring into space, Stefanie finally said, "Well, come to think of it, a few times I picked up that they were actually having fun. They did all laugh in that group shot. And when she almost fell, that was interesting."

"Very. There's more to that relationship than either one is willing to share. Or admit." She returned to her tasks and they finished within a few minutes.

Once in the elevator Stef commented, "But then Kate made a big deal out of Jason and practically crawled all over him. Jason seemed stunned."

"I know. I wonder how much of that was for Mother's benefit. It gets curiouser and curiouser."

CHAPTER FIVE

The gathering of the new site committee came to order that evening. Laurel had put their mother in a room on one of the lower floors with a promise to join her for dinner with Stef and Kate afterward. Her mother insisted that Dasher be included and tried to also invite Jason, but he told her he had plans. Kate was relieved, because her mother would thoroughly embarrass both of them by putting Jason through an inquisition.

Kate wasn't looking forward to their dinner plans, and evidently neither was Dasher. She thought Dash was about to bolt when Mrs. Hoffman insisted and Stef gave her a look that only good friends could get away with. She had to laugh. Stef would definitely owe Dasher a lot for what she'd put her through today.

Kate was pretty sure Dasher hadn't volunteered for the photo shoot, judging from her obvious awkwardness in front of the camera. Kate couldn't imagine why, because the angles on Dasher's face were made for the camera. And the way she wore the leather cat suit—well, anyone would have reacted to that sight. Kate was positive she wasn't the only one who got a bit short of breath when she realized it was Dasher wearing it.

Only Seraphina's booming voice brought her back from her musing. Irina Castic and Seraphina Holloway presided over the meeting, and nine others were present. Laurel and Stef, of course, and Kate sat with them. Conn Stryker and Leigh Grove, her partner, had volunteered to help because they knew the northern California coast and were researching locations. Their adopted sister from Pakistan was there, too. Zehra? Kate thought that was her name. The three of them seemed fresh and full of ideas. Kate was envious because her day had been long and confusing and draining. The only good part of it was that Dasher Pate wasn't here. A slight reprieve before dinner was helpful.

A few other members rounded out the group. Just as they were quieting down to begin, Dasher silently entered and sat at the back of the room. Kate's heart sped up and stopped, all at the same time. *Great. Can it get any worse?*

"Ladies." Seraphina brought them to order. "Irina told the entire group about the main purpose of the project. But another element has been proposed. Miss Kouros-Stryker, would you care to explain to us?" She gestured to the young Pakistani woman, who suddenly glanced around shyly and then looked pleadingly at Conn Stryker.

Both Conn and Leigh gave her reassuring nods and she stood, appearing almost overwhelmed that the group was waiting for her to speak. After clearing her throat twice, she began.

"In my country, and in many developing nations, women are regularly enslaved and abused. 'Corrective rape,'" she used her fingers to make quotation marks, "for women who are suspected of being lesbians, is not just a phenomenon in Africa, but used as an excuse to humiliate and abuse women in many countries. Poor women are forced to become breeders, sex slaves, prostitutes, or indentured servants and have no chance of escape. They are kept illiterate and forced to wait on males their entire lives and put to death if they dare rebel. Sometimes they are worth less than the animals they tend."

She paused to look around and seemed encouraged by the silence and rapt attention. "I propose that once we establish our property, we bring some of them to the land and teach them how to read and write, and how to manage for themselves. We can also teach them a trade, if they desire, or let them attend school if they want. Most of all, they need to feel safe and capable of guiding their own lives."

Her large hazel eyes were shining when she abruptly sat down, and Leigh Grove quietly took her hand while Conn Stryker put her arm around Zehra's slender shoulders.

Kate was stunned. Why did she know nothing about this? Her world was so full of things that revolved strictly around her. She had always chosen to avoid anything that threatened to be unpleasant, and her looks had helped her succeed.

One of the members, the interior designer of the hotel, as Kate recalled, was a beautiful woman with large dark blue eyes and collar-length blond hair, shot with some white streaks. Kate thought her to be in her late forties. She asked in a gentle voice with no judgment in her tone, "Zehra, are the women you want to bring to our new compound all from one particular country? Are they all lesbians?"

Conn answered, her gaze completely focused. "It's impossible to know what orientation these women are. They've been so brutalized I doubt they know. While there are several in particular who helped us escape from Pakistan, the list is long and the process to get them admitted to the United States is arduous. Our plan is not to limit by country, including the United States, or orientation, but to accept because of history and experience. Our Elysium members in the State Department and other areas of the government have pledged to help. They will work from their end. Our job is to locate and purchase the land and have it ready for our first arrivals. That's why we couldn't put this off until after the hotel opens."

"What's the next step?" The rich alto voice was Dasher's. Kate and everyone else turned to the sound.

Sika Phelps, Denny's mother, her accent a melodious reminder of her West African heritage, said, "We have assembled a list of available properties located within three hours of the hotel that we might purchase and make into our next location. The list is long and we need to narrow it to three or so. If all of you can spare a few weekends to do some investigating, we'll split up the list and report back in three weeks' time with recommendations."

Everyone nodded, but Kate could tell Stef was uncomfortable. From their dinner conversation the night before, she knew Stef had so many responsibilities with the hotel, this would be a hardship for her. Without thought, she canted to get closer to her and said, "Don't worry, I'll take your list. I have time now." The look of astonishment mixed with gratitude from Stef made Kate smile. She knew she wasn't exactly known for being generous with much more than money. Well, that was changing, thanks to Mrs. Roosevelt.

Truthfully, she wasn't comfortable volunteering her time to do God knows what. But she had to do one thing every day that scared her. She decided that *uncomfortable* was another word for fear, though to a lesser degree. Besides, Stef was probably teamed with Laurel, so this project would be simple and give her more time with her sister.

Irina had been conferring with Laurel and called for their attention, pieces of paper in her hand. "All right, let's set up the teams. Carolyn and Ember, you'll handle the South Bay, around Half Moon Bay and Pacifica, down to Carmel and Carmel Valley. Conn and Leigh will handle the North Coast up to Eureka. Stef and Dasher, you'll proceed to the Wine Country. I know, a difficult duty." The others groaned their envy but, actually, it was all wine country. She was probably referring only to Sonoma and Napa counties, more inland.

"Laurel and Kate, you'll handle the East Bay. There's a lot of land to cover. Zehra and Sika are our floaters. In the short time Zehra has been in the United States, she's become a technology aficionado and will be researching for us via the computer, as well as going to sites that might be possible candidates and evaluating them. Zehra, you and Sika will also keep track of everyone and their reports, and fill in when someone can't make it for whatever reason. Okay, are there questions?"

Laurel stood and was taking questions, but Kate didn't hear a word. Somehow her big mouth had just dumped her from the frying pan into the fire. She would be working with Dasher Pate on this project. She hadn't thought about who *she* might be teamed with, and she hadn't yet snapped to the fact that Laurel wouldn't be on two teams at once. *She* was now on two teams and she couldn't turn either one down. They needed her. She had time to do this while her knee mended.

Maybe Dasher didn't have the space on her calendar that she did, or maybe she would refuse to work with her. Maybe her earlier bitchiness would pay off in the form of Dasher asking for another partner once she found out hers would be Kate. That thought was strangely depressing, but Kate had long ago learned to push such emotions into the "unexamined" file and leave them there. Her recent musings were only because she'd been sidelined by her injury. Really.

"Stefanie said you wanted to be my partner for the search. Is that true?" Dasher's voice vibrated in her ear, and Kate steeled herself to look at her and try not to be insulting. After all, she'd gotten herself into this mess.

Meeting Dasher's gray eyes momentarily disoriented her. Suspicion was there, yes, but also something else. Hope, perhaps? This situation took her promise to herself about doing frightening things to a new level.

She heard her voice shake as she said, "Well, I said I'd take on Stef's part of the search because I have more time now, between projects. I didn't realize she would be with you." Dasher did an about-face to leave. "Wait, Dasher, let me finish."

Whirling back to her, Dasher spat, "If you want to deliver another piece of clever sarcasm, save your breath. I'll find a replacement on my own."

Rushing before Dasher could get away, Kate said, "I just wanted to say that I look forward to it. It will be…an adventure. Right? Besides, we have to get the property purchased if we want to help those women. So we'll just have to put aside our differences. I apologize if I've been difficult. Shake?" She impulsively stuck out her hand and realized too late that touching Dasher Pate was a mistake.

When their hands joined, the spark and snap made her flinch. "Oh! The carpet, it must have…" She was only vaguely aware that she couldn't move her mouth.

Dasher quickly said, "Yeah, the carpet. Well, um, I'll get our lists and then we can look at our schedules. Would you like to do that tonight or tomorrow morning? I have to return Greta to the set in LA tomorrow afternoon." Thank God, Dash was looking at Laurel, who was handing out the lists of possible properties, and not her. Kate feverishly tried to gather her wits.

Laurel glanced over and said, "Sorry, girls, but I promised Mom we'd have dinner with her tonight. That includes you, too, Dasher." Laurel winked at her.

Looking somewhat desperate, Dasher said, "You know,

I realize you two want to be alone with your mom. So, Kate, breakfast tomorrow?"

It was late, and Kate was exhausted. Her knee hurt and her head was close to meltdown with too much sensory information. She needed to be alone. Fat chance.

"I have to get back to LA, too. Yeah, breakfast. Say, eight o'clock? I'll meet you in the lobby. But you're coming to dinner, aren't you?" With Dasher there, maybe she could duck the inquisition her mother was sure to conduct about Jason Beresford.

Dasher cocked her head and seemed to relax. "Okay. Dinner. And breakfast for the list. Perfect."

Half an hour later they were in the café listening to Marilyn Hoffman talk about anything and everything. Dasher watched and listened to the family interactions. Stefanie was new to the Hoffman family, too, but she was Laurel's partner, and Marilyn always included her. She also filled Dasher in on details of the girls growing up and talked a lot about her son.

Several times Kate or Laurel would chastise her for telling embarrassing stories, but their chiding seemed good-natured. Mrs. Hoffman appeared to have a generous nature and to love her children dearly. Dasher envied the easy banter among family members. They seemed to trust each other.

Over dessert and coffee, Marilyn casually said, "Well, I wanted you to know that I'm leaving your father."

Dasher stilled and looked around. Stefanie was the only other one staring.

Stirring a bit of cream into her coffee, Kate offhandedly said, "Again?"

"This time I mean it. He's an old curmudgeon. Never

wants to go anywhere, do anything. Just wants to work and putter in that damned garage. I left him a note this time."

"So Daddy knows you're with us." Laurel put down her fork

"Well, yes, where else would I be?" By her tone, Dasher guessed she wasn't a party girl.

Laurel seemed a bit exasperated. "Mom, why don't you talk to Daddy? I'm sure he's fine about you visiting us without him. I know he tunes out a lot, but you don't have to leave permanently."

"Well, he just ignores me. I've talked 'til I'm blue in the face and he won't take a vacation."

Laurel shot a desperate look at Kate. Sighing, she said, "He's agreed to come for the opening of the hotel. That's something. Maybe you can extend the trip and take a cruise that leaves from San Francisco." She returned to stirring her coffee, as if that should be the end of it.

"Hey, I have an idea," Stefanie said. "Beresford Hotels has a great property in Hawaii in Kona, on the Big Island. It has individual units over the water or on the beach, and they provide all the meals. You can snorkel, sit on the beach, whatever you like. I'll bet I can get a deal for you and you can fly over right after the opening. How's that?"

"That sounds wonderful, but I'm not sure he'd leave his precious couch and garage for mere beaches. My only other idea was to go down and spend time with Kate. He does love to go to the set and watch Kate and the technical people work. Kate, would you be upset if we went to Hawaii instead?"

After the words came out of Marilyn's mouth, the spoon Kate was using to stir with picked up so much speed the coffee slopped into the saucer.

Laurel immediately said, "Great idea, Stef! I'll research

flights tomorrow. Mom, you and Daddy need to spend time with each other, away from us and work and garages. You get him to agree and we'll do the rest. Right, everyone?"

Dasher found herself nodding vigorously. Impulsively, she offered, "I can arrange a tour of my father's training facility. He has a school to train stuntmen and women in Kona. If you don't want to go, I'm sure your husband would enjoy it."

Marilyn's eyes lit up. "That might be just the thing that gets him to go! He loves those car chases and explosions. Thank you, Dasher."

The relieved expressions on both Laurel and Kate's faces were comical. They quickly finished dessert, and Laurel and Stef escorted Mrs. Hoffman to her room.

Standing at the Elysium elevator, Kate said, "Thanks, Dasher. You might have saved the day."

"You're welcome. I like your mom. She just sounds bored. I was glad to help."

Kate was very close to Dasher as they spoke. Dasher's eyes were so warm, her husky voice so inviting, that Kate impulsively hugged her. Dash was still, then her body softened and she returned the hug. It felt too good.

"So, Kate, I'll see you tomorrow morning and we can go over the lists. Okay?"

Dasher had such a genuine quality. Stepping back, Kate managed to say, "Um, yeah. Eight o'clock. Well, good night." She swiped her card, pressed her hand to the plate, and the elevator arrived within seconds. Although Dasher was joining the Elysium Society, she'd told them she'd keep her room on the lower floor until she could find time to get her card and the hand scan done.

The elevator doors closed to the image of Dasher's smile.

Kate fled to her room and packed her bags. Within minutes she caught a cab to the airport and was in Los Angeles by midnight.

CHAPTER SIX

Kate stood staring at her traitorous telephone ten days later. What good was it anyhow? After taking the coward's way out and flying home, she and Laurel had a blowout argument over the *phone*. None of Kate's normal theatrics that she successfully used to get out of her own screwups had worked on Laurel. She told her that she'd better make it right with Dasher and hold up her end of the bargain to Elysium. Now she had to call—again, the *phone*—Dasher Pate and admit she'd made a complete ass of herself. She was not looking forward to it. Kate cursed her own impulsiveness once more. Nothing good could come of volunteering.

To top it off Laurel, the rat, had sent the proof sheets from the photo shoot. Probably just as a not-too-subtle reminder of the whole fiasco. She threw the envelope on her desk unopened. She didn't need another guilt trip.

After exercising, showering, returning calls, doing laundry, and signing about a million publicity photos to be sent to fans, which she could have easily let someone on her staff stamp, she couldn't come up with anything to put off the call once more. Laurel had pointedly given her Dasher's private number, thereby eliminating another stall. She stabbed in the numbers and held her breath, praying it would roll to voice mail. No such luck.

"This is Dasher."

The silence was unnerving. Finally, Kate managed, "Hi Dasher, it's Kate."

When no reply came, she huffed. "Kate Hoffman. Remember me?" Her nervous laughter was embarrassing.

After a moment Dasher said, "Yes, I do. You're the woman who breaks promises. I keep falling for it and you keep doing it. Silly me." Her tone wasn't angry, just without emotion. Kate would have preferred anger.

"Look, I wanted to apologize for skipping out on you in San Francisco. I just had to get back to LA sooner than I thought." *There, perfectly plausible.*

"You were in such a hurry you couldn't have left a message for me at the desk, or called, or e-mailed, or told Laurel or Stef?"

Without much conviction Kate replied, "Yeah, that big a hurry. I…apologize."

"You know, you don't have to do this search project. I can do it by myself. If you're just apologizing to placate Laurel, I'll get you out of it. Let's not make each other miserable."

The low rumble of Dasher's voice and her offer of a way out disturbed Kate. She hadn't thought about how her behavior was making Dasher feel. "Do you have time to go up this week? I promise I'll show up. I don't know why I always seem to… Anyway, I'd like another chance." She could have taken Dasher's offer to chicken out, but that didn't seem like an option right now. Kate hoped she wouldn't regret her decision.

After a hesitation, Dasher said, "I'm going to San Francisco Thursday. Sika called and has a lead on some property up the coast, and Conn and Leigh are in DC for some meetings. I'm not sure you'd even be interested. It's—"

"Of course I'm interested. What time should I meet you?"

Dasher seemed irritated. "What I was going to say, Kate, was that it's raw land. We'll have to camp out, at least for one night. By ourselves."

"Camp out? As in, tents and campfires and…bugs?" Kate couldn't help it. Bugs.

"Yes."

Kate thought she heard a challenge in Dasher's tone. *Damnit.* "No problem. Are you flying up?"

"I'm driving. I want to take my own equipment and four-wheel drive vehicle. In case the roads are difficult. Do you want a ride?"

Too quickly Kate said, "No. I'll just meet you there."

"Fine. Ten a.m. on Thursday at the hotel. See you then."

Kate was sure she heard skepticism in Dasher's voice. As in, *I bet you don't show up.* She'd painted herself into quite a corner and now she had to put up or shut up.

Joe would be furious. He'd done nothing but complain about the time she spent at the hotel anyway. She didn't dare mention that she'd volunteered for this project, let alone that she'd be within three miles of Dasher Pate. For some reason he had a real button on Dasher. The man was so aggravating.

Well, if he was going to be so pissy, she wouldn't tell him. She'd say she had decided to go to Tucson to Canyon Ranch to get in touch with her spiritual side. He would roll his eyes and that would be the end of it. Someday she'd actually have to go to the place. He thought she was practically a shareholder.

Now she needed some camping gear. She looked up the nearest REI and hopped in her Mercedes SLR McLaren Roadster and was there in minutes. Two hours later she barely made it home with all the crap the drooling salesman had talked her into. She realized too late that a roadster and camping gear didn't match. Although it had a trunk, not much fit into it. It was probably designed to hold shopping bags, maybe a picnic basket. That's all she'd used it for.

Though she was tempted to call Dasher again and ask her to haul the stuff with her when she drove, she couldn't bring herself to do it. She'd have to pack an extra duffel or two and pay a bunch for this trip. Dasher told her they'd be spending only one night camping, but she forgot to ask if one night was all they'd be away. She needed to be prepared for anything.

❖

Kate was glaring at Dasher's back as she deftly assembled her tent. Hers lay in shambles ten feet away. She knew damned good and well that Dasher was enjoying her ineptitude.

She watched the well-defined muscles in Dasher's forearms work, fascinated by her strong hands as she expertly hammered stakes in the ground. Dasher erected her tent within minutes, complete with a foyer thingy in front. Such competence irked her.

Sighing heavily, Kate glanced over her shoulder at the mess she'd made and begrudgingly admitted, "This camping stuff is new to me."

Dusting off her hands, Dasher stood back and examined her own tent. She was gloating, Kate was sure of it. She was grinding her teeth but tried not to show her irritation. She needed help or the tent was not going up, and she wasn't about to either sleep in the open or beg Dasher to let her share her tent. No way.

"Would you like some help?" Kate couldn't detect condescension in the question, but knew it was there.

In exasperation, she blurted, "Yes, of *course* I need help.

Those idiots at the sporting-goods store said this one was the easiest to put up, but obviously they were wrong."

Dasher covered her mouth with her hand, like stroking a beard. She eyed the pile of poles and nylon and made a noncommittal grunt. "I see. Well, you chose a free-standing one, no stakes or anything. As long as there's no wind or rain, you should be okay. Does it come with a ground tarp? First, you separate the poles from the material. Then you read the directions. Did you try that yet?"

The woman was incorrigible. "For your information, I am a college graduate and the stupid directions were written in Chinese or something and that moron at the store said it was so simple *anyone* could do it. Then he had the nerve to want a picture of me. I should have made him come out here to put the stupid thing up."

Dasher shook her head. "No. Then I'd have to deal with a man slobbering all over you the whole trip. I'll help you."

Finally getting the answer she wanted, Kate smiled. "Good. While you're doing that I have to, um, use the facilities. Where are they?"

Dasher gave her a long look. "Kate, we're a distance from any actual plumbing. You've probably noticed that fact."

"Well, we're not *that* far. Half-hour max, right? Give me the keys, I'll drive." Kate really needed to go and this was simply barbaric. "And while I'm at it, maybe I'll find a hotel and meet you tomorrow."

Dasher's expression seemed condescending. Kate snapped, "What is your problem?"

Dasher ground out, "You. You're my problem. When we met five years ago you seemed like a talented, down-to-earth woman. You've turned into a fucking prima donna. Look at you. You even wore makeup to go camping, for God's sake. Would you like me to build you a spa? As it is, I have to set up your tent and cook for you. You don't even have the decency to act like you want to pitch in and help. You *expect* to be waited on."

Digging in her pocket, Dasher found the car keys and tossed them on the ground. "There. And you don't need to bother coming back. Jock and Denny will be here tomorrow, and they'll give me a lift after we look over the property. I'm sure you need to get back to LA for a manicure or something important. I still can't figure out…" She sighed and turned to stare into the woods that were about a hundred feet from their clearing.

Kate resisted the urge to snatch the keys off the ground, race to the car, and peel out of there, leaving Dasher in the dust. That would have been her usual escape plan. Instead, she dug her heels into the ground and slapped her hands on her hips. "What can't you figure out, Miss I'm So Cool and You're a Piece of Crap? I don't know how to camp. So what?"

Sighing deeply, Dasher turned and met her eyes. "I just thought that out here, where it's so beautiful, so quiet and peaceful, out here maybe I'd catch a glimpse of the woman I met before. I was wrong. I apologize. I can't ask you to be something you're not." Her shoulders slumped and she studied the keys on the ground before picking them up and offering them to Kate. "Here. You shouldn't have to do anything against your will. Come back tomorrow if you want to. If not, I'll understand."

Kate hated to see the disappointment in Dasher's eyes. She had gotten her way, after all. Wasn't that the most important thing? She felt terrible. Dasher's words stung all the more because Kate knew she was right. She was behaving like some of the actors she detested. But Dasher wasn't right about everything. Kate was *not* like those others. She had to prove that, if only to herself.

"No, I said I'd do this and I will. I just… Do we at least have any toilet paper?" When Dasher only nodded, she said, "What do I do with the tissue after I'm, um, through?" She knew she was blushing, judging by the heat rising up her neck to warm her face, and she still wanted to run. But for some ungodly reason, she couldn't.

When she dared to look up, Dasher was grinning. Her heart seemed to skip a beat, or some such cliché, she was so pleased to see the beauty of that smile. Her reaction to it unnerved her.

Dasher said, "You have two choices: one is to, er, drip dry. The other is to use some biodegradable toilet paper and enzyme packets I have in the SUV. Take the camp shovel to bury it. If you have to do more, you'll need to dig a deeper hole and then sprinkle some enzyme packets over it after you finish, including the tissue. The idea is to not leave a human footprint. If we do this again I'll buy a camp toilet for your convenience."

The reference to future outings together oddly pleased Kate. Dasher's gentle tease gave her a choice: truce or another tantrum. She was tired of arguing with Dasher and she really had to pee. "Deal."

She stuck out her hand to shake and when Dasher took it, the warmth immediately vibrated throughout Kate's body. *Ah, short memory, Kate. You should know better.* Her breath caught and belatedly she tried to cover her reaction with a cough that forced her to pull away to cover her mouth. She *had* to remember not to touch that woman. She still thought about their hug at the hotel.

"I'll need that shovel and biowhatever stuff." She was barely croaking out the words, but Dasher seemed not to notice. Except for the slight rose hue on Dasher's face, Kate wouldn't have guessed she had any reaction to the touch.

"I'll be right back." Dasher stuffed her hands in the back pockets of her jeans, along with the keys, and took a moment to locate the SUV before wandering toward it.

"I'll need it soon!" Kate kept her voice singsongy, but her words seemed to get Dasher in gear. Within fifteen seconds she had what she needed.

Pointing toward the edge of the forest, Dasher said, "Don't go too far in, because it's dense in there and easy to get lost."

"No problem." She snatched the articles from Dasher and fled into the woods.

❖

Twenty minutes later Kate was using the back of the shovel to pat down the dirt of the hole she'd just filled in and feeling quite smug about her success. "Well, guess I've got what it takes to go camping after all. Now I'll go back and put up my tent. All I needed was a little—" She stilled when she heard a snuffling sound behind her. It was close to the ground, followed by a whine.

Whirling around, she spotted a tiny white puppy sitting on the ground not five feet from her. It backed up, apparently frightened by her size. She quickly crouched and put the shovel behind her to appear less threatening.

"Well, hello, little one. What are you doing out here? Where's your mama, hmm?" The creature enchanted her, and Kate instantly worried about it. Holding out her hand, she said, "C'mere, sweetie. You're shivering. I'll warm you up and we'll find your mother. I'll bet you're hungry."

The little pup wobbled over to her and sniffed carefully, then plopped again. It allowed Kate to pick it up, and she quickly peeked enough to know she had a soft, fuzzy little boy snuggling into the crook of her arm.

"You are so precious." Hearing some crashing through the underbrush, she smiled in anticipation of showing Dasher her find. She froze when a large dark animal appeared, sporting tusks.

"Jesus." It must have weighed over 400 pounds. It studied her with little pig eyes and lifted its snout to sniff. A boar or something. The puppy whined and buried its head again, trembling.

Mustering up all her courage, she slowly stood to her full height and yelled, "Shoo!" It didn't move. Indeed, it took a step closer, having seen the white pup. She swore it licked its chops. *Aren't pigs vegetarians?*

Kate reached behind her and felt for the small shovel she'd propped against a tree trunk, hoping to brandish it and scare the creature away. It took another step and she pulled back. Its eyes never left the puppy.

"No. You can't have him. Now leave." It snorted and pawed the ground, its body tensing as if to lunge.

Reasoning that if the pup was out of sight the pig would leave, and she would probably need both hands to frighten the creature away, Kate carefully opened her shirt. She placed the pup inside next to her skin and buttoned the shirt, making sure it was secure and tucked tightly into her pants, keeping her eyes on the pig. The puppy settled immediately, and Kate even registered a tiny tongue tasting her skin.

"Now, you. Go away." She tried to look huge to the boar, but it just cocked its head at her. "Well, this isn't working, is it? I swear it did on TV."

Something about the creature wasn't right. It bristled and seemed to grow in size, and Kate belatedly realized she'd probably just challenged the damned thing. "Oh, shit!" She took off as fast as she could.

Crashing through the underbrush in what she hoped was

the direction of the camp, she screamed, "Help! Help! Wild pig!" She could hear even louder thundering behind her and suddenly realized that if she found the clearing, the boar could hurt a surprised Dasher. She veered in another direction and looked for a low-hanging branch, ignoring her protesting knee.

Making sure the pup was secure under her shirt, she spotted a tree and branch that looked reachable and headed for it. She yelled, "Hold on!" to the pup and leapt, managing to snag the limb with both hands, then swing a leg over it and hoist herself up. She quickly checked her passenger, who seemed fine, pale eyes regarding her with complete trust.

The hog was at the bottom of the trunk, snorting and pawing. Kate carefully scooted closer to the trunk of the tree where the branch was thicker and rested against it, sighing in momentary relief. Now to get out of here. "Help! Someone bring me a gun!" She was thinking of an elephant gun when she heard more noise in the underbrush and saw Dasher emerge, wielding a baseball bat, eyes frantically scanning the area.

"Kate! Kate, where are you?" She skidded to a halt when she spotted the boar. "Holy shit."

"Up here. Dasher, be careful. We're okay, it can't reach us."

Evidently needing to see for herself, Dasher glanced up. "Us?"

The hog snorted and got Dasher's attention and they squared off, Dasher trying to poke at it with the bat. It didn't run away.

"Dasher, get up here. That thing is crazy."

Shaking her head slightly, Dasher said, "I don't think the branch will hold me, too. Can't risk it breaking. Pray for a home run." She assumed a batting stance, bat moving loosely in her hands, eyes fixed on the huge animal's head.

"Dasher, no! It'll rip you to pieces." Kate frantically searched for another tree that Dash could jump into, but nothing big enough was nearby. The puppy wiggled in her shirt and whined, then yawped.

Behind Dasher and the pig a flash of white tore out of the underbrush and attacked the boar. The animal fought to grab the hog's throat, its huge teeth ripping and tearing. Kate watched in terror as Dash tried to help by distracting the beast to bash it without hitting their white protector.

Kate heard a humming sound and then the beast roared, stood motionless, and dropped, an arrow sticking out of its ear. It seemed like the forest was stunned to silence. Nothing moved.

It wasn't until Kate's little visitor whined again and started wiggling inside her shirt that the white dog looked up and was suddenly on its feet, snarling at Dasher. She watched helplessly as Dasher took up the bat that she had let hang in her hand.

"No!" Kate waved furiously to distract the angry animal.

"Blanca. Stay." The cultured female voice came from the right of Kate and Dasher. The dog immediately sat, still growling and restless.

A tall, slim woman with snow white hair that dropped well below her shoulders stepped into the open. Her face was tanned and her eyes the color of the sky on a gorgeous spring day. She held a powerful-looking bow, and a leather sheaf of arrows was strapped to her back. Although she was wearing cargo pants and a blue denim work shirt, Kate flashed that leathers might have been more fitting.

Dasher was panting. "Why is she mad at me? What did I do so I can stop doing it?" She still had her bat at the ready.

The woman came a few steps closer, an arrow strung lightly in her bow. She cautiously examined the boar and, evidently satisfied that it was dead, loosened the arrow and put it with the others.

Finally looking at Dasher, she said, "Blanca thinks you have something that belongs to her. One of her cubs is missing."

The pup chose that moment to stick its head out of Kate's shirt and yawn. Blanca tensed and started growling.

Kate sputtered, "I'm sorry. The puppy came to me and was scared, and then the pig appeared and seemed like it wanted to eat the poor thing. I stuffed it in my shirt and ran. I wasn't trying to steal her puppy, I swear."

She moved to get down and lost her balance, falling a few feet only to land in a heap with Dasher on the bottom and the pup unscathed. She quickly unbuttoned her shirt so the little guy could scramble over to his mother. Blanca sniffed him, licked him, eyed them, then grabbed the pup by the scruff of his neck and loped out of the clearing.

The woman strode over to Kate and gave her a hand. She was taller than Kate and hauled her up effortlessly. A small smile played across her lips. "I guess we should thank you, then, for saving her cub. She was frantic."

"Cub? He's not a dog?"

Dasher struggled to her feet and huffed. "I think maybe that makes her a wolf. Jeez, Kate, I thought you just went for a walk."

Then Dash gingerly examined the dead boar. "Thank you for rescuing us. Were you bow hunting?"

Shaking her head, the woman said, "Blanca and I were looking for her cub. I don't use a firearm. This boar has been terrorizing the local farmers. It killed a lamb recently. I knew it was out here."

Kate edged close enough to look at the kill and shuddered. "He…I…excuse me." She sank to her knees.

Dasher dropped the bat, and she and the woman helped Kate up. Kate clung to Dasher.

The stranger said, "I'd better be going. My name is Diana. I'll send someone to fetch the boar. He won't go to waste."

Dasher offered her hand. "I'm Dasher and this is Kate. Thank you so much for saving us."

Kate was about to say something when the woman nodded slightly and then turned. She left as quietly as she came.

Kate finally stood back, releasing her grip on Dasher. Dasher held her eyes with tenderness, then her gaze dropped and she suddenly examined her bat and the boar. Kate wondered why until she looked down. Her shirt was almost completely open, her lace bra revealing a lot of flesh. She turned and buttoned it up, then tapped Dasher on the shoulder.

Dasher was blushing such a bright pink that Kate felt a smile tugging at the corner of her mouth. "Well, I guess it's a good thing I took care of my shoveling chores before the cub appeared. That boar scared me to death and I would have really humiliated myself. Thank you. I think I almost got you killed."

Grinning, Dasher said, "Nah. Maimed, maybe. Come on, let's go make a campfire. I have your tent almost up."

"Where did the bat come from?"

Snapping to a batter's stance, Dasher said, "I played for my college team." She dropped the bat head and rested on it, grinning. "I lettered."

At that moment big drops of rain made Kate and Dasher look up, and Kate groaned, "What next?"

Dasher grabbed her hand and pulled her along. "Don't ask, we don't need to know."

They laughed and ran all the way back to the campsite as the skies opened up. Kate couldn't remember the last time she'd felt so free.

❖

They arrived at the clearing just in time to see Kate's tent blowing toward them like a tumbleweed. Scrambling out of the way, they had to duck and zigzag to dodge flying pieces of equipment. When they reached Dasher's tent, she heaved Kate inside the vestibule and held onto her belt so she didn't do a face-plant on the floor. She followed Kate, then zipped them inside. They were soaked.

Looking around the vestibule and realizing it was dry, Kate said, "Wow. This is cool. Now what?"

Dasher was apparently making sure everything was tightly secured as the wind buffeted the walls of the structure.

Finally turning to Kate, Dasher hesitated, then said, "Take off your clothes."

Kate froze as approximately five hundred thoughts and emotions ran through her mind. Hesitation, fear, calculation, lust, suspicion, trust—they were all there. After taking a nanosecond to firmly delete "lust," she registered the wind again. The knifelike cold ran through her because of her soaked clothes and she started to undress.

The rush of adrenaline that had gotten her through the ordeal with the boar was fast wearing off. Her hands shook and her teeth chattered as she tried to unbutton her shirt in the cramped space. Usually, if shooting an action scene where she had to be in water, she was helped by dressers and quickly warmed up with a hot shower and fuzzy robe and slippers. Out here in the middle of nowhere, she was on her own and not faring that well.

"M-mm-my shirt." You'd think as many times as she'd buttoned and unbuttoned the stupid thing today it would be easy, but the wet material and her shaking hands were making it impossible.

Then the strong hands she'd secretly admired only an hour before were there, deftly releasing the material and peeling her out of the shirt. Dasher had her mouth set and her gaze focused as she immediately reached behind Kate to release her bra clasp. Kate knew her eyes must have widened in the universal expression of surprise, but Dasher didn't meet them.

Instead she reached inside the tent and pulled a flannel shirt out of her duffel, holding it in front of Kate. "Take off your bra and put this on. Hurry, you're too cold." She averted her eyes and Kate numbly let the bra drop and slipped into the shirt. Its softness and the subtle scent she suspected was Dasher's told her it was a much-washed and probably much-loved favorite.

As good as the shirt felt, the adrenaline surge from the run-in with the boar had left Kate shaking even harder. She observed more than felt Dasher gently remove the rest of her skintight version of LA outdoor clothing as she helped Kate navigate into the roomy sweatpants and warm socks.

Dasher stripped out of her top and, clad only in her sports bra and jeans, searched inside the main part of the tent to retrieve a camp towel. She fussed with Kate's hair, evidently trying to wring out as much moisture as she could. Kate allowed it, held captive by Dasher's tight body, the defined muscles under the silky-looking exterior. She remembered the puppy tasting her skin and had the urge to do something similar. *You must be losing your mind.*

Finally, Dasher half dragged her into the main portion of the tent and carefully stuffed her into a sleeping bag. She studied Dash as she checked the tent for leaks and fiddled with the bag, tucking here and there.

Their eyes met briefly before Dasher crawled to her duffel and grabbed a pair of flannel shorts and wiggled out of her jeans, having to work hard to push the wet fabric off her long legs in the confined space. Dasher was sculpted and toned and perfect. Kate watched the concentration on her face and was struck by her own feelings of tenderness.

She was warm enough now to throw back the top of the bag and help, but she didn't. She couldn't assist without touching Dasher. And once she touched Dash, she would be lost.

A shiver ran through her as she saw, as clearly as if it had been projected on the big screen, that all of her work for the past five years was at risk. Joe had warned her to stay away from Dasher, so he must have known, too. He'd said that associating with Dash would destroy her career. Dasher was jealous of his success as an agent and was trying to poach her as a client. He also told her that Dasher was unscrupulous. But after five years of working with Joe, Kate suspected she knew who was unscrupulous, and it wasn't Dasher Pate.

Dash finally settled next to her, the two of them forced to share the sleeping bag. Kate closed her eyes and feigned sleep, something in which she was an expert. She longed to face Dasher, to tell her how brave and strong she was, to thank her for her kindness. To kiss her.

She rolled to face the tent wall, feeling tears form in her eyes and terrified Dasher would see them. She couldn't, wouldn't, let her see her weakness. Most of all, she couldn't let her see what others probably did. She cared for Dasher Pate, and nothing good could come of it.

Chapter Seven

Kate awoke to the sensation of being walked on and licked. She jerked her eyes open from a rather erotic dream to see the white cub from the day before, his pink tongue giving her nose a thorough cleaning. Not wanting to disturb his ablutions, she tried to look around for Dasher while holding still. Then she heard Dasher's laughter outside and several other female voices. *What the hell?*

At that moment the cub decided to chomp down on his newly cleaned catch, and Kate yelped as loud as she could without scaring her captor. She and the cub were having a stare-down when Dasher stuck her head in the tent and smiled disarmingly.

"Good morning. We have visitors."

"So I see, and hear. I'm a mess." For some reason she didn't feel shy about looking a fright around Dasher, but strangers made her uneasy.

"It's okay. It's the huntress and Luna and, ah, I see you and Squirt have already gotten reacquainted. Jock Reynolds and Denny Phelps arrived at about the same time she did. You look beautiful, come on out." Her eyes confirmed her words and made Kate defy her instincts and decide to appear almost as disheveled as she was.

"Do you at least have a brush I could run through my hair?" After all, there were limits.

Dasher rummaged through her duffel and produced one that was obviously not intended for long hair, but it was that or nothing. After some concerted brushing that produced a lot of electricity, which had the pup jumping around her lap thinking it was great fun, she emerged to find all the women chatting amiably.

Conversation stopped as they stared at her. Her courage faltered and she put Squirt down, thinking maybe she could slip back into the tent, claiming to have forgotten something.

Denny said, "You were right, Dasher. She's even more dazzling without makeup."

Kate glanced up to see that all the women were smiling in welcome. *Dasher said that?* She straightened up and Squirt immediately yawped to be held again, trying to climb her pant leg.

They must have realized the clothes weren't her own and that she and Dasher had slept together. Well, not *slept* together, but slept in the same tent. In the same sleeping bag. When she vaguely remembered tucking herself into the curve of Dasher's body sometime during the night, her cheeks started to flame in earnest.

The others evidently didn't notice because they resumed their conversation, but Kate could still feel the heat from Dasher's body when she'd slipped an arm over her waist and pulled her closer, as if they were made for each other. No wonder she was having an erotic dream when she woke up. If she were being honest, that dream involved a woman's body, not a man's. That had happened before. But this time, the body had a face, and the owner of that face was now chatting amiably three feet from her.

"Okay, we'll clean up the campsite and gather what we

can find of Kate's tent and head over to your place, Diana. I'm betting Kate would run me down to get to a hot shower. Is that right, Kate?" Her tease was light and friendly.

"A hot shower? Yes, I'd drive over you and back up, if that's what it took. Thank you, Diana. Were you able to haul that creature away?"

Diana nodded, while Jock and Denny were silent but were probably curious. "I sent several of my employees over last night, or the forest creatures would have it finished by now. I came to invite you and your friends to the celebration. We'll serve the boar and many other dishes, since a lot of the residents up here are vegetarian. Everyone's glad to have that beast gone from terrorizing the livestock. They'd be happy to meet you."

After Diana said her good-byes and left, Jock and Denny started peppering Dasher and Kate with questions about the "creature." Soon, they were all laughing and teasing Kate about screaming "pig" throughout the forest.

As Kate watched the interactions, she started to relax and feel more comfortable with these two very tall women. They seemed so natural together. Laurel had told her that they'd known each other since they played college basketball on the same team. Jock had a sturdy build while Denny was thin and graceful. They definitely had that peaches-and-cream and café-au-lait thing going—really attractive. Were they a couple?

She'd always clung to Laurel or Stefanie when she was around them, and now here she was, making her own friendship with them. She'd already filled her scary quota for the day.

With some bravado she marched to a closed plastic box and secured the necessary items for her morning ablutions. Somehow in the dash back to the tent, she'd managed to snag the shovel and toilet paper. She had her priorities. She was a camper.

❖

Michael was pouting in the car, refusing to help. Chaz determinedly jumped on the freaking jack they'd found in the back of the crappy rental car. No luck. It wouldn't budge.

Chaz had insisted on following Reynolds and Phelps when they left the hotel, sure they knew where Kate and that Pate woman had snuck off to. How had he and Michael missed them? They were only slightly buzzed the day before, but when they returned to their vigil at the hotel they saw Pate and Kate Hoffman drive past them. It was too late to run back to their rent-a-wreck. So much for Chaz's attempts to save money.

Chaz knew what most of the players in the hotel looked like by this time. He'd identified them over the past month while Kate had been visiting. When Denny and Jock claimed Jock's truck at four in the morning, he followed. Now this.

Michael had bitched the entire time. He was getting more vocal about this whole assignment. He had no idea how much potential money was involved. Well, Chaz had no such qualms. This was going to put them on the map. Michael just didn't understand about finances.

Now this freaking flat tire that he had no idea how to fix. A rumbling behind him on the curve signaled potential help. He prepared to try to wave the guy down but froze when he recognized Jock Reynolds's truck. Holy crap!

They pulled over and Jock stuck her head out the window. "Need any help?"

Trying desperately to look friendly instead of guilty, Chaz stole a glance in the car at Michael and saw his eyes like saucers in surprise and, yes, guilt. "Yeah, the jack is worthless on this rental car. We're stuck."

Jock had exited the truck and was studying the disabled

vehicle. "Well, for one thing, you're trying to use the jack on an incline. That's pretty dangerous. Have you called a tow truck?"

Chaz lied. "Dead cell-phone battery." He shrugged and said, "When it rains, it pours, eh?"

Pulling a phone from the case attached to her belt, Jock made the call. Chaz was at once relieved and irritated. He would have thought of that eventually. Denny Phelps stepped out of the truck, and the two of them looked like Amazons coming to the rescue. Although he envied the look, they dwarfed him and Michael, which made him uncomfortable.

Denny conferred quietly with Jock and then made another call. After a brief conversation, during which Michael managed to find his balls and drag his butt out of the car, Denny extended her hand for them to shake. "Hey, I'm sure it'll take a few hours to repair your car. Why don't you come with us to a barbecue? I just asked and they've extended the invitation. We can take you to the garage afterward. Sound like a deal?"

Oh my gawd, this is just too good. It was like Kate Hoffman was being dropped in their laps. "Sure, right, Michael?" He gave Michael a look that told him to just nod.

Ignoring him like he usually did, Michael said, "We won't know anyone. Are you sure? We don't want to intrude."

Chaz held his breath, silently vowing to strangle Michael if he blew it for them.

Denny smiled. "Oh, you might recognize a face or two. Come on, you'll have fun."

She was so genuine that Chaz momentarily forgot he was on a job. He was almost in the backseat of the extended-cab truck before he remembered that they would need a camera. He was trying to come up with a plausible reason to return to the rental when Michael joined him in the backseat, two cases in his arms.

"I don't want to risk losing our stuff when they take the car." He smiled sweetly and they just nodded, because the tow truck had arrived. Within a few minutes they were on their way, and Chaz elbowed Michael and winked at him. He certainly had his moments.

❖

Kate didn't want to waste time getting the camping site in order. Dasher scoured the area for any of their debris tossed around by the storm the night before and took down her own tent while Kate packed the Porsche SUV. It was surprisingly roomy and she loved making everything fit. Maybe she'd rethink her next car purchase. Dasher nodded approval before they set out for the offer of hot showers. Kate couldn't wait.

She read the directions aloud to Dasher and anticipated seeing some small ranchette with chickens in the yard and a tractor in the field. She was more than a little surprised when they arrived at a gated entrance with several fellows checking a list for their names. Diana's last name was Tartaglia. Evidently in these parts that translated to "owns a bucketload of land."

As they drove in, Dasher asked, "Have you read the list of the properties we're supposed to see? I think a Tartaglia parcel is among them. If not, I'd be surprised."

They traveled for three minutes before the house came into view. Rather, the hacienda, complete with tile roof and gorgeous grounds surrounded by fruit orchards. Kate would bet there were some olive and fig trees, too. The place was bustling.

Dasher gave a low whistle. "Whoa. I guess the film industry isn't the only way to make a buck. Come on, let's see if we can find Diana, then dig our clothes out of the back of the car."

After asking one or two people, they located Diana directing traffic for those setting up the feast. The cooking pork smelled divine, and Kate went to look, just to make sure the boar was still dead and it really had happened. There the huge thing was, on a large spit, rotating as a man basted it. She shuddered.

A warm hand on her shoulder told her Dasher had followed. “Don’t worry, the brute’s harmless now.”

Kate reflexively held Dasher’s hand in place and put her cheek on top of it in thanks for the reassurance. She told herself to not nestle into Dash’s body, that it would be too much. Luckily Diana waved them over and they were preoccupied with her for a bit.

At the door to her own suite she faced Dasher, not sure what to say. While they were by themselves it was easy to let her guard down and just enjoy being with Dash, but soon they would be among people who would only recognize her as a persona with whom they had very little in common. That façade was all she had to protect herself from strangers. Dasher had proved that she wasn’t a part of the façade. She could be trusted.

“Well, I guess I’ll see you downstairs, less smelly than now. Hey, thanks for rescuing me yesterday and sharing your tent. That was nice.”

The look of kind acceptance on Dasher’s face was too much for Kate, and she gently touched Dasher’s lips with her own, then fled to the safety of her room, quickly closing the door.

❖

The party was well under way when Kate emerged from the house and strolled to the sprawling backyard of the estate.

People were laughing and eating, evidently in a celebratory mood.

Kate was back in her LA uniform—tight black jeans and expensive boots with a long-sleeved, V-neck, plum-colored spandex top. Her makeup was in place, as was her smile. She searched the crowd for a familiar face, her anxiety increasing until she saw Dasher and made eye contact. That smile made it possible to breathe until she registered the familiar sound of a camera's shutter.

She located it and saw several more, mostly from folks with either camera phones or small personal digital models. Two men standing close to Denny and Jock made her radar ping. One was taking photos rapid-fire with a very expensive Nikon. The other was smiling and ducking his head slightly. She even wondered if she'd seen them before.

Diana was by her side in the next moment, with Dasher in tow. She announced to the group that these were the two that helped her capture the rogue boar, and the listeners all applauded. Someone shouted, "Thank you!" from the crowd, and good-natured laughter was widespread.

After the announcement, a line of sorts formed, of the kind that Kate had seen before. She would probably be signing autographs soon. To her surprise the people wanted only to thank her and Dash personally. By the time they were through Kate felt like a superheroine, and Dash was standing quite tall herself. During that time the fellow with the Nikon kept taking shots.

After a few minutes the other man appeared before her, next in line. He shook her hand lightly and bowed just a bit, never making eye contact. "You were very brave," he said. "I probably would have fainted."

She smiled, immediately liking the shy Asian man. "I would have but I didn't have time. I took one look at the tusks on that thing and just started running."

He bowed again and moved to shake Dasher's hand. The next she saw of him he was by the photographer, speaking animatedly with him. The man shrugged and put the camera down. She was very glad to be dressed as she was but hoped those photos edited out Dasher, because Joe would have a fit. She was sure the two men were professionals and wondered where they'd come from.

An hour later, after a wonderful meal of dishes that many of the locals had prepared, and only a taste of the boar, Denny came over and rescued Kate from several of the admiring teenagers who were there with their families.

As they walked over to Diana, Jock, and Dasher, Kate asked, "What's up?"

"Do you ride horses?"

"Yes. I really enjoy it. Why?"

"Well, Dasher and Diana have gone over your list and discovered that Diana owns one of the pieces of property on it. She's offered to show it to us, but the shortest way is by horse. Jock and I don't ride, and I have no desire to learn unless it's really necessary. Dasher said she could go with Diana, and we were wondering if you could, too. Two sets of eyes on this would be better than one."

Delighted to be away from the crowd and have another semi-private moment with Dasher, Kate immediately said yes. She even picked out her mount, a gorgeous buckskin mare, and saddled her while getting to know her. She loved talking to horses because they seemed so wise. By nature, they were discreet.

Suddenly aware of being watched, she whirled to see Dasher, holding the reins of a huge black stallion. She smiled and said, "I see you and your horse are good friends. Spitfire and I haven't quite gotten to a first-name basis yet." She looked skeptically over her shoulder to the horse, who was pawing the ground and snorting.

"Spitfire? Do you ride, Dash? What I mean is, he looks rather spirited. Where's Diana?" Kate knew by looking at the horse that it needed an experienced rider.

"Out front, saying good-bye to some of her guests. Denny and Jock plan to stay until we return, and I found out that they were the ones who brought those two guys with the cameras. Picked them up on the road when they had a flat tire. So that means they'll be around, too."

Kate knew she was scowling when she said, "I'm guessing they're paparazzi, Dash. What were they doing up here?"

"My thoughts, too. But I don't think they were around our site, because they don't seem to have a clue about anything that involves camping. The smaller one, Michael, told me they came up early this morning. Maybe it was just coincidence." Dasher was watching her, studying her reaction.

As if reading her mind, Dash added, "We didn't do anything wrong, Kate."

Too quickly, Kate said, "It's just, you know how photos can be turned around and twisted to tell made-up stories. Joe would… Never mind. Let's go see the property. They aren't invited to do that, are they?"

Diana answered. "Hell, no. That blue-eyed fellow almost devoured the boar by himself. They can wait with Denny and Jock. They'll keep an eye on them."

❖

Chaz watched the three women head off on their horses, trying to figure out how to follow them. How far could it be, anyway? But Reynolds and Phelps were sticking close, acting suspicious of him and Michael.

When Reynolds got a call on her cell, she walked away

from their awkward little group and had a somewhat agitated conversation. She rang off and hurried over to them, announcing that some load of carpet or paint or crap had been delayed by an accident with a truck. They had to get back right away.

Immediately, Chaz said, "Go on. Don't worry about us. The guy at the garage said they could come and get us if we needed them."

Looking doubtful and stressed, Jock nodded curtly. "I'd better not see any pictures from today in the papers. I mean that." The look she gave each of them made Chaz break out in a sweat.

She and Denny tore out down the driveway, leaving them staring.

Dusting his hands together, Chaz said, "Hokay! Got rid of them. Not very friendly, if you ask me. Now, where's my camera and which way did they go?" He batted his eyes at Michael and grinned.

Putting his hands on his hips, Michael pursed his lips. "No way. You're on your own. I'm not running after a group on horseback, for God's sake. You heard Jock. We can't even use the shots we got today. Let's just call the garage."

Slipping the strap of the Nikon with the telescopic lens already mounted on it over his head, Chaz started loping in the direction he'd seen Hoffman and Pate head. "Our employer will decide what ends up in the papers, not Jock Reynolds. I'll be back soon—with the goods!"

A mile out and three fences later, Kate and the other two horsewomen halted at the top of a ridge. They were surrounded by scrub oak and the brown hills of California.

"How large a parcel is it?" Dasher had brought her PDA and was taking notes as her mount grazed peacefully. She loosely wrapped the reins around the pommel of the saddle.

"Three hundred acres, five of which are developed. It was originally supposed to be a resort. Luxury cabins with a main lodge were ready, but before it could open, the developer tanked and the property reverted to me." Diana consulted a piece of paper from her shirt pocket.

"The roads are roughed in for the whole parcel and the resort is pristine, complete with a well. The septic system is state of the art and the lodge has a professional kitchen. Everything so far is mostly run with solar. It came back to me like that."

Beyond the ridge, the Pacific Ocean stretched endlessly before Kate, a rougher, more raw version of her view from Malibu. A fresh breeze bathed her face. She took a deep breath, savoring the crisp ocean air. "This is beautiful. It seems ideal. Dash?"

Looking up from her notes, Dasher said, "How much do you want, Diana? For everything."

Diana seemed to consider the question. "I want to know more about this Elysium Society Denny mentioned. Then, if this is the right place for your plans, we'll talk."

Just then, they heard a growl and then a scream and turned in their saddles to see Chaz Hockaday fighting his way out of a grove of scrub oak and blackberry bushes with Luna hanging on to the seat of his pants.

"Help! I'm being attacked!" He swiped ineffectually at Luna, who seemed more playful than serious, but nonetheless held on to him and shook her head, bouncing Hockaday around.

Spitfire reared, and Dasher barely stayed on. Her PDA

went flying into the scrub. Spitfire pranced and bucked, then settled.

Diana called, “Luna, release.”

Luna immediately let go of Chaz and left him to pick the blackberry vines off his body and clothes and untangle the camera from the detritus he’d been hiding in. Luna sat placidly a few feet from him. Kate thought Luna seemed amused.

Diana eyed him. “Mr. Hockaday. You have been my guest this afternoon. Is this the way you repay my invitation? By spying on my friends?”

Evidently trying for innocence, Chaz said, “I was just… out for a stroll. Miss Tartaglia, I would never—”

“Save it, Hockaday,” Diana said. “We’ve already guessed your motives. You’re on private property and don’t have permission for photos. By the way, that was poison oak mixed in with the blackberry thorns. Now get moving.”

Hockaday’s eyes went round. “Poison oak? I’m really allergic to that stuff. Oh, my God!” He started frantically trying to untangle himself, which only compounded the problem because the blackberry vines were scratching and cutting him.

“Freeze!” Dasher’s voice was so commanding that all of them stopped moving.

“You’re making it worse. Diana, I hate to ask, but may I borrow, er, have your riding gloves? I’ll pick the stuff off of him. I’m allergic, too, and I know how miserable it can be if—”

“I’ll do it,” Kate said. “When I was a kid I used to practically roll in the stuff and never had a reaction.”

Nodding, Diana said, “We’ve got some antihistamine pills and salve we can give him. That should be enough to get him to the emergency room.”

Kate dismounted and marched over to Chaz. "I should let you suffer. Don't move." He stood meekly as she slipped into Diana's riding gloves and carefully picked off the brambles and poison oak vines. His arms, face, and neck were already a mass of welts and scratches.

Ten minutes later she stood back and examined her work. "We'd better get him on my horse, his face is swelling."

Chaz croaked, "I itch and I don't know how to ride a horse." He looked miserable but clung to his camera.

"Ride behind me, Kate." Dasher offered her hand and slipped her foot from the stirrup so Kate could use it.

Kate nodded. "I'll hold his reins, we better hurry."

They set off for the hacienda at a trot, Chaz bouncing up and down and periodically groaning. He had a death grip on the saddle horn.

As far as Kate was concerned, hugging Dasher and leading the buckskin was a mixture of heaven and hell. Dasher was in great shape and she rode as if she was one with Spitfire. Listening to Chaz reminded her why she couldn't explore the relationship further.

An hour later they had treated Chaz as best they could. A ranch hand loaded him and Michael into a truck to take Chaz to the hospital and drop Michael off at the garage for their car.

Grateful and very worried about Chaz, Michael apologized and waved as they pulled away from the house. Kate got the impression he cared for Chaz quite a bit. She hoped his taste in men improved.

As the truck disappeared around a curve, Dasher began to swear. "My PDA! I lost it when Spitfire reared, then forgot about it. Damnit, it has my life on it."

Diana was just coming out of the barn. "The horses are settled, why don't you take the RTV? I've had it modified with an electric engine so it won't disturb the animals. You have about an hour until sunset and you're welcome to stay the night. It's late to head back. That location has beautiful sunsets, by the way."

She regarded Kate with wise eyes. "You go too, Kate. Two will have better luck finding it than one. I'd volunteer, but I have a lot of work to do." She smiled so innocently that Kate was nodding without one warning whistle sounding in her brain.

Entering an outbuilding beside the barn, within a minute Diana produced something called a Kubota. Unlike the ATVs Kate was familiar with on the sets of some of her films, this one was almost silent and had room enough for two on a bench seat. It reminded her of a really macho golf cart.

Pointing, Diana said, "Just follow the trail back and you should easily find the area where Mr. Hockaday met his big bad wolf."

Dasher glanced at Kate. "Thanks. I could use the help."

Now the klaxons were blaring. It was risky to be alone with Dasher Pate.

Dasher smiled shyly. Just then Kate felt a pressure on her leg. She looked down and there was Squirt, wanting to be held. After she swooped him up she nuzzled his furry face. "Diana, can he come, too?"

Shaking her head slightly, Diana said, "Maybe next time. Luna would feel the need to follow, and she's tired. It's almost his dinnertime."

At the mention of the word "dinner," Squirt began to wriggle in her arms and Kate put him down, watching as he scampered after Diana. "I feel so cheap. Turned down for dinner with his mother."

Dasher hopped in the RTV, pressed the ignition, and said, "If it makes you feel better, he's still nursing."

"Oh." Kate needed to think about that.

The RTV wasn't fast but bumped along at a steady pace. The electric motor kept it quiet, and Kate could sit back and enjoy the ride.

"How's your mother?" Dasher asked. "She's very proud of you two. You especially."

Kate was quiet. "I guess so. I used to feel guilty. Around our house it was always about my brother, the male, and me, the star. Even when I was little, Laurel was almost ignored because she was quiet. She was lucky."

Dasher cast her a sideways glance. "What do you mean?"

When Kate had made this remark before, most people scoffed and assumed she was just angling for compliments about how talented and beautiful she was. Others always thought they knew what she was thinking. Dasher was the first who seemed actually curious.

"Laurel was able to go her own way. She went to college, got her doctorate, and taught. What she wanted to do. I'm sorry she hooked up with the woman before Stefanie, because they weren't good together, but our parents didn't put up much of a stink even when Laurel told them she was a lesbian. They said, 'Oh, that's just Laurel.'"

"I guess it was different for you." Dasher kept her eyes on the trail and Kate was grateful because the words came more easily.

She sighed and watched some of the black-tailed deer that were venturing out in the waning day. "Oh, yeah. Kate the model, Kate the dancer, Kate the homecoming queen. Kate the celebrity, Kate the star. Little-Miss-Perfect Kate."

"Did you have a lot of friends?"

Trying to keep the bitterness from her voice, she said, "No. I had people who liked to hang out with Kate the Fill-In-the-Blank for a little reflected glory. The moment something better came along, they were gone. I guess I was training for Hollywood."

"What about Laurel? I didn't get the feeling she was jealous of you."

"Laurel's my best friend. I'm so glad she's happy."

Dasher was quiet. "You don't sound happy."

"I *am* happy…for her." Kate's eyes stung and her chest burned. She couldn't say more. Besides, she had nothing to whine about. She didn't even know if Dasher was trustworthy. She seemed like it, but she worked in Hollywood, too.

It took thirty minutes to reach the section of trail that was littered with brambles and vines. Diana had provided another set of heavy-duty gloves, and Dasher looked for her PDA while Kate gingerly cleared the trail to prevent anyone else from getting tangled.

"I can't find the freaking thing. I had it in my hand, and then Hockaday screamed like a banshee and Spitfire reared. I thought it went this way, but nothing. The undergrowth is pretty thick."

Finishing her task, Kate removed her gloves and tossed them in a box on the back of the tractor, straightened, and looked around. Shadows were making it hard to see. "Does it have a cover? I honestly don't remember it."

Shifting her weight to one hip, Dasher sighed. "No. I'd been meaning to get one. A neon green one. Well, let's—" She took a step and they both heard a crack. "Shit." Looking down, she found her PDA under her left foot.

Kate covered her mouth with her hand and snorted. "Oops." At first Dasher scowled at her, then seemed to be trying hard to be angry. Eventually they were both laughing.

Dasher picked up the device, its screen thoroughly ruined. Kate tried to console her. "Well, you probably have most of it backed up, right? And we can get the property information from Diana again."

"I guess." Dasher just kept staring at it, probably trying to will it whole again.

Kate suddenly remembered Diana's words. "Hey, have we missed the sunset?"

They looked toward the ocean and could see the sun as vibrant orange, sinking quickly. But the water wasn't visible. Instead, the sun was disappearing into a thick layer of gray-blue fog. Kate half expected to hear the hiss from its heat as the froth and moisture cooled it. The quiet that surrounded them, the light sea breeze, and the last rays of the warmth of white heat being absorbed by the fog made the spot seem magical.

Standing close to Dasher, Kate stopped breathing, wanting to capture every second of the moment, wanting to share it. Dasher took her hand as the dusk gathered around them. Kate turned to her and reached to touch her face.

She heard the sharp intake of breath as she ran her thumb over Dasher's lower lip, sensing more than seeing that Dasher kissed the tip of her thumb. It seemed so natural to slide her arms over Dasher's shoulders and pull her close.

Halting just inches away, Kate searched Dasher's eyes and saw something she'd never seen before. She closed her eyes but it was too late. Too late to stop the kiss, too late to control her body and the yearning.

The kiss deepened and Dasher held her tight. But it was Dasher who finally broke the spell. "Kate? Is this what you want?"

Kate searched her eyes. "What's wrong? We're alone, no one can see us. Don't you want it, too?"

"I think you know the answer. But is this all we'll have?"

Kate had just kissed, really kissed, a woman for the first time in her life. Wasn't that enough? She was reeling with all of the emotions at war in her body, not to mention the alarms clanging in all lobes of her brain.

"Dasher, can't we just have our moment? Can't we have something we'll never forget? You know what it's like in LA. What my job is, the expectations. You, better than anyone, *know*. What are you asking?"

They touched foreheads. "Nothing. We'll have this moment, then, and that will be all." She gently kissed her lips once more. "We'd better get back. Squirt will be looking for you."

Once at the ranch, by unspoken consent they made their excuses and drove back to the Bay Area. Squirt had tried to come with them and Diana had to chase him and hold him as they drove away. Kate knew she'd done the right thing for both of them by stopping what her body and heart ached for. She didn't want to hurt Dasher more than she just had. Damned beautiful sunset.

But the look on Dasher's face mirrored her own misery and only served to add one more piece of kindling to the smoldering resentment she had for her life in Movieland.

CHAPTER EIGHT

Dasher dropped Kate at Hotel Liaison after their silent return and sped away. Kate watched her car until it disappeared around a corner. Dasher's expression, what she thought of as a mixture of regret and aloofness, was one she wouldn't forget soon. It left her feeling empty.

Kate limped inside the hotel and made her way to the bar. She didn't know what time it was, but it had to be after 5:00 p.m. somewhere in the world, and she needed a drink.

It was quiet, just a few tables with women dressed in downtown professional attire looking like they were talking business. The lighting was muted and no one paid attention to her as she found a booth in the darkest corner of the room.

After a moment Ember Jones appeared and asked her for her order. Lord, was there a job in this joint she didn't cover?

Morosely, she replied, "A new life."

Ember laughed nervously, obviously not knowing what on earth Kate was talking about. Kate envied the young woman her clean slate. Ember was just starting her life, and hopefully she wouldn't mess it up by chasing illusions.

Taking mercy on her, Kate mustered a small smile and said, "In lieu of that, how about a Maker's Mark Manhattan, straight up, two cherries." *That's right, Kate, old girl. You're about to splurge and have two cherries. Calories be damned. What a daredevil you are.*

She was quietly shredding her cocktail napkin and eating a few pretzels when someone placed her drink in front of her. "Can I get you anything else? A shoulder to cry on?"

The voice belonged to Laurel, and when Kate met her concerned expression, she chose to study her drink. "Let that waitress of yours know her tip just evaporated. What did she tell you?" The women around here sure weren't very good at discretion, even though Kate knew she wouldn't end up looking like she felt in a tabloid photo.

"Ember was worried and thought maybe I could help. Besides, you obviously didn't notice who was behind the bar." Gesturing toward the cocktail, Laurel said, "Try it, I've been practicing. Even make my own bitters." Laurel was grinning, which always helped lighten Kate's moods.

Kate sipped and the drink went down so smoothly, she sipped again. "That's good, Laur. If the hotel business doesn't work I think you've got a career as a mixologist."

"Slow down, tiger. It has a kick. Our regular bartender just came on duty, so I'm off. You want company?"

No. "Okay." As Laurel went to check out, Kate added, "And bring another one of your specials back with you. My story is long and boring, and I need to hop a flight back to LA tonight."

Five minutes later Laurel placed two Manhattans on the table. "Sounds like I'll need one, too."

Glumly, Kate asked, "Where's Stef?"

"Having dinner with Jason. They never get to be alone, so I sent them off to have some fun. I'm so glad I did because you and I seldom have time either. What's up? I thought you were with Dasher, looking at property."

The mention of Dasher's name brought the last few

days and hours back with a resounding thud. "I was. And we found one that looks really promising." Laurel started to say something but Kate just plowed ahead. "A lovely woman whose name happens to be Diana owns it. She's a huntress with bow and arrow who saved our lives when a giant boar charged me and Dasher tried to help and I was trying to rescue a cute little wolf cub we call Squirt that I thought was a puppy and I kissed her." *There, it's all out. I feel better now.* She wondered if she'd slurred any words.

Laurel sat quietly for a moment, then carefully took a swig of her drink and cocked her head. "Kissed who? The cub, the huntress, or Dasher?"

"Weren't you listening? I kissed Dasher. I couldn't help it. I think it was the sunset."

"The sunset. Did she kiss you back?"

Just above a whisper, Kate replied, "Yes."

"And you liked it."

The effects of the alcohol must have loosened her tongue, because the truth spilled out. "I've never had a kiss like that. I felt it in every cell of my body and in places that I… Yeah, I liked it a lot."

Laurel cleared her throat and started shredding her own napkin. Kate idly wondered if napkin shredding was genetic. "Well. I didn't know you liked women, Kate. You've never mentioned it. Have you ever been with a woman before?"

"Of course not! I mean, not really. In high school I did some experimental kissing with Naomi Harris. This thing with Dash. It was just a…a…one-time thing or something. I don't have time for this complication in my life. *Been* with a woman? Listen, Professor, if that's a fancy way of asking if we slept together, no. It was only a kiss. Just a kiss." She determinedly started on her second drink.

Holding her hands up in surrender, Laurel said, "Okay,

okay. Just a kiss. When you told Dasher that's all it was, what did she say?"

Kate played with the pretzels. "She agreed. I mean, she said okay. Then we drove back here and she dropped me off. She's on her way back to LA."

"Oh." Laurel sipped thoughtfully.

Irritated, Kate drained her glass and said, "Spill it, Laurel. You're thinking something and you'd better share." She really didn't want to know, but her damned mouth just kept running.

Placing the stemmed glass carefully on the table, Laurel said, "Well, Kate, Dasher is a lesbian. From what Stef tells me, she's a nice person, too. No one wants to be someone else's experiment. Not even the great Kate Hoffman's. Now you tell me, did you kiss her just to see what it was like? Or did you kiss her because you felt something for her?"

"Shit." Kate seriously considered a third Manhattan.

Patting her hand consolingly, Laurel said, "Come on, I'll help you pack and order a limo. You have some thinking to do."

Chapter Nine

It was a long drive back to Los Angeles. Dasher set the cruise control to 85 miles per hour as soon as she was across the Bay Bridge and on her way to Highway 5 and a straight shot down the coast. She cranked the sound system, avoiding the sadder songs of McLachlan, Cassidy, and Raitt. Not caring if she got a ticket, she raced down the road.

The whole idea of being around Kate Hoffman had been foolish. She should never have joined the Elysium Society, never volunteered to be on the same committee. She was like a damned moth to Kate's flame. Maybe she was only starstruck.

"Yeah, Dasher, starstruck with her beauty. Like you haven't had about a dozen women as beautiful throw themselves at you. Well, not that beautiful, but it's still a lie."

If Dasher had learned one thing, it was that she couldn't have what she wanted, craved. Dasher was a caregiver. That's how she'd survived her childhood and that's how she made her living. But that street ran only one way. Her worth was as a care*giver*, not the other way around.

She vowed to never again acknowledge her true feelings for Kate, especially to herself. It was a dead end and only kept her from finding someone to have a real relationship with. She absolutely wouldn't pursue this any longer. If Kate insisted that they remember the kiss but indulge in no others, then so be it. She'd just have to figure out how to do that and move on.

Close to midnight someone rang her and the hands-free system picked up the call in the car. "Hey, honey, have you talked with your mother in the last few days?"

"No, Dad. I told you I'd be out of town until tomorrow. As it is I'm back a bit early. Lupe needed to take care of her granddaughter while her daughter was on a business trip, and you agreed you'd handle Mom. Two days, Dad. Did you even bother to call her?"

Her mother was an emotional train wreck, and her dad didn't want to deal with her. So he let Dasher handle all of their baggage and had since she was a child. She only occasionally asked him to help, and this is what he did. She half expected it.

"Now, Dash, don't use that tone with me. She's a grown woman, she can look after herself for a few days." Ah, the best defense is a good offense. One of his favorites.

"She's not well, Dad, and you know it. I was out of town for two lousy days. Did you call or not?"

Sounding every inch a petulant and quite spoiled teenager, her father said, "Of course I did, just a few minutes ago. I don't think she picks up when I call. She's just being stubborn."

Goosing the accelerator, Dash shot toward Beverly Hills instead of her own home in Malibu. Her father, Jerry, had purchased a condominium in a fine old refurbished building and plunked his wife there. She could have everything delivered and watch big-screen television and drink and pop pills as much as she wished.

As soon as Dasher escaped to college in the East, her dad

had moved his wife out of their Beverly Hills digs. He paid her bills and gave her a stipend and washed his hands of her, expecting Dasher, their only child, to take care of the rest. After two near misses that involved breaking down her door and paramedics, and Dasher ferrying between coasts, Dasher had transferred to UCLA and lived at home. Dasher now had her mother's power of attorney for medical and legal affairs.

Mimi Pate was a desperately unhappy woman who had arrived in Los Angeles as a sixteen-year-old runaway and married the first man who proposed. Since she had refused to ever speak about her parents, her father in particular, Dasher assumed that Mimi had been abused.

It was probably just dumb luck on Mimi's part that she didn't pick another abuser as a mate. It was lucky for Dasher, too, because as irritating as her father could be, he loved Dasher and provided for them.

Young Jerry Pate became a much-in-demand stuntman and traveled all over the world on location for films. He told Dasher that at first he tried to take Mimi with him, but she was terrified of flying. When Dasher was born, Mimi wouldn't be parted from her, and he went his own way.

Now, as the top second-unit director in Hollywood and owner of the best stunt-performance school, Jerry was wealthy. He wasn't unkind, just checked out. He immersed himself in work and threw money at a problem that had started long before he met beautiful, dark, and sensitive Mimi.

Her painful shyness had eventually made her a virtual shut-in. She had no friends and relied solely on Dasher to provide comfort. The burden had become increasingly difficult to bear.

Each time she couldn't reach her mother and was working, she called the caregiver who visited Mimi and shopped, cooked, and cleaned for her. Guadalupe Correa, a middle-aged woman from Ecuador, was now on a full-time salary. Dash had also provided her with a cell phone and helped her purchase a car.

Lupe turned out to be a compassionate woman who always helped if she could. Dasher tried to be generous at holidays and any time she could come up with a reason to give Lupe more money, because Lupe wouldn't accept what she called "tips" and, so far, wouldn't take a raise either.

Between caring for her mother and representing her growing number of clients, Dasher didn't have room for much else. Dating was a joke, more like one-night stands. Lately, she didn't have much energy for even those.

She managed to find a place to park on the street, no small feat in that neighborhood at four in the morning. It was quiet, with only a few nocturnal critters making their nightly rounds, foraging. She let herself in the main door and walked up two flights to her mother's flat, avoiding the creaky elevator.

Her mom kept odd hours. She often watched old movies all night because she had a hard time sleeping. Dash planned to make sure she was okay and then go home. After the past thirty-six hours, what were a few more without sleep?

As she let herself into the unit, she heard the ever-present noise of the television. It was on constantly and quite possibly kept the monsters away. Dasher's heart rate elevated and she was holding her breath. She always dreaded what she would find when she came over.

There, on the couch, sprawled Mimi Pate. She was passed out and had vomited on herself. Dasher quickly checked her pulse and found a steady if weak one. Next, she made sure her airway was clear. With a speed born of practice she called the paramedics and tried to clean her mother up before they arrived.

Waking at the interruption, her mother groaned, "Just let

me die. Why can't you leave me alone? I just want to die." It was always the same.

"Mother, the ambulance will be here soon. Just hang on for a little while longer." When Dasher was a kid, she'd watched the movie *They Shoot Horses, Don't They?* All she could remember was that in the end the guy had killed the woman because she was so very damaged by a dead-end life. She'd stared at the television, her mother passed out on the floor, long after it ended.

She remembered wondering if she would have the courage to grant her mother's wish to die. But try as she might, she couldn't. Nor could she follow her father's lead and leave.

She managed to stuff her mother into a clean top, like dressing a rag doll, and heard the siren of the approaching emergency personnel. A fire truck always accompanied them, for some odd reason. The neighbors had long ago stopped coming out to see what was happening. She suspected most just slept through the commotion by now.

In the beginning one or two had bitched about the episodic disruption. Then first her father, and now she, would supply them with tickets to movie premieres and they stopped complaining.

Even the reporters who haunted the police and emergency scanners rarely showed up these days. People stopped thinking it was news.

She made a mental note to give a generous donation to the paramedic and fire department funds when this calmed down. Holding her mother, who was crying, in her arms, she waited.

❖

The next morning Kate was leaving her physical therapy date across the street from the hospital, only slightly hungover.

She could barely drag herself to the stupidly early appointment. Luckily, the incident with the boar hadn't reinjured her knee, but her therapist had scolded her and warned her yet again not to overdo it. Yeah, like she'd had a choice.

Ambling to her car she muttered, "Yes, ma'am, I'll try not to let a wild pig chase me from now on."

She halted when she thought she spied Dasher, still wearing the same clothes she had on the day before, sitting outside the hospital on a bench. She was staring into space and looked exhausted. Kate stood still while buses and cars zoomed past, attempting to make sense of what she saw.

Ignoring her revving heart rate, she watched as Dasher slumped forward, elbows on her knees, and put her face in her hands. She seemed so vulnerable, so hopeless. Kate forgot about her complaints, and her feet moved without actually asking permission.

After she crossed the street, she quietly joined Dasher on the bench. "Are you okay?" Scooting closer, she gave Dasher some time to decide if she would engage. She was prepared to be told to go away, but fervently hoped it wouldn't happen.

Dasher stilled, then sat up and gazed at Kate. "What are you doing here?"

Kate tried for nonchalance. "I had physical therapy across the street. I saw you and thought…I thought maybe you could use a cup of overpriced coffee. Can I buy you one? There's a Peet's down the street, and you know how hard they are to find in LA."

Dasher hesitated, then smiled slightly, fatigue lining her face. "Yes. I'd like that."

"Come on, then. The morning rush should be over." She donned her large sunglasses, her attempt at disguise when alone, and they walked together to the coffee store two blocks down. "My treat. You want a triple shot?"

Dasher grinned sadly. "That bad, eh? I guess it's a good idea. Might get me to my car and home without falling asleep."

"And a scone. Two scones. I feel like cheating after the torture that PT put me through."

"Careful. Don't let Joe catch you eating carbs."

"He could do with a few less himself." Kate was relieved to have Dasher at least attempt humor.

"The difference is you work out and he owns stock in Krispy Kreme."

Dasher sat outside and Kate stood in the short line, anxious to get back to her. The young man who waited on her stared but had the good sense to not ask if she was really Kate Hoffman. She gathered up her goodies, and as she used her shoulder to push open the door she noticed him pull out his cell phone.

"Hey, why don't we walk back to the hospital? They have a garden in the center of the complex that's private. I think the coffee dude is Twittering, and you know it won't take long for others to show up."

"Sure. I have to get back anyway."

They walked until Kate couldn't contain her curiosity any longer. "Dash, why are you at the hospital? Can I help?"

Every time she was around this woman she started doing things she'd rarely done before. Offering to go out of her way for a friend was something with which she had little experience.

Dasher seemed to consider the offer, then tiredly shook her head. "It's my mother. She tends to drink too much and take too many pills. Then I get to find her and call the paramedics and here we are. It's happened before."

Kate could only nod. She'd heard that Dasher's mother had some problems. Joe was always happy to comment on how screwed up Dasher probably was because of it.

"Have you slept yet?" From the look of her, Kate doubted it.

"I dozed in one of those comfortable waiting-room chairs in the emergency room. No, not really."

"Is she well enough to leave? Do you want me to drive you home?"

Gazing at Kate as if trying to decide something, Dasher finally said, "Mom is agoraphobic. I asked her internist to run some tests on her because she's lost a lot of weight recently and Lupe told me she's been having some, as she would say, lady troubles. More than usual, that is. This is the only time doctors can get a crack at her. They're keeping her for forty-eight hours."

At that moment a tiny, sturdy square of a woman hustled up to Dasher, who stood to accept a fierce hug. The woman was speaking Spanish rapidly and Dash seemed to get most of it. She patted Dasher's arm and disappeared through the hospital doors with barely a glance in Kate's direction.

To Kate's unasked question, Dash said, "That's Lupe, who takes care of Mom most of the time. She's a godsend. She's my relief for the day shift."

"Isn't your mother safe in the hospital?"

Dash shook her head. "My mother is terrified of strangers. She'll be okay with Lupe or me in the room."

"What about your father?" Kate knew who he was. Jerry Pate was quite sought-after in her circles. If you wanted a stunt done right and the first time—and often these action sequences took months and cost millions to choreograph and film—you hired Jerry Pate.

Snorting, Dasher said, "Not likely. He's got all sorts of reasons why, but other than paying her bills, he might as well be her ex. I guess my dad doesn't ask for a divorce because then other women can't pressure him to get married and he gets to maintain control of his money. Nice."

She rubbed her face and sighed deeply. "Well, I've got to get going. I have two appointments today and I can't look like this, for my clients' sake. Then I can try for some sleep before I come back here to the hospital."

"If you need anything, please call me. I mean that." Kate had no idea *why* she meant it, but she did.

After a moment, Dasher simply replied, "Thank you." Kate knew she wouldn't call.

Driving home, Kate pondered her reaction to Dasher's terrible situation. She was outraged that Jerry Pate had handed over the care of his wife to their child.

Why was she feeling so protective of Dasher? Sitting with her in the garden, she had to force herself not to pull Dasher into her arms to comfort her, give her a safe place to let down. She wondered how often Dasher actually did that—allowed herself to be vulnerable in front of someone else. She knew how often she'd felt that safe. Never.

Even around Laurel, she thought she had to keep up the charade her family had created and she had always done her best to live up to. The Gifted One. The conversation she'd had with Laurel the night before, when she was half drunk, was the closest she'd ever come to spilling the truth. Kate was tired. She longed for shelter from the storm that was the essence of fame and celebrity.

CHAPTER TEN

Dasher took a break at the same time each morning for the next two days, on the same bench in the inner garden of the hospital. Each morning Kate miraculously appeared, bringing coffee and scones. Dasher gave up trying to feel one way or another about Kate's companionship. She simply enjoyed it for what it was: an act of kindness.

Perhaps if they could only have one kiss, they could at least be friends. Perhaps that would be okay. She was beyond even venturing a guess.

The second day as they sat in the garden, Kate asked, "Is your mother going home today?"

"Today or tomorrow. Lupe's already up there. Mom will get her test results, and since I'd never be able to get her to the doctors' offices to hear them, Lupe will call me when the docs arrive." She checked her watch absently. "They seem to be running late today. I need to hear the results, too, because Lupe doesn't speak English well enough to either understand what they say or explain it all to me in detail, and I don't trust Mom to remember everything."

Kate smiled. "So, you just came down to hang out?"

Dash studied her coffee. "Yup. Just to hang out and see if maybe the scone princess would make my day."

"Well, I'm glad you're here. I've enjoyed seeing you." She sounded as mystified by their meetings as Dasher was.

"Kate, would you like to meet my mother?" Kate's expression made Dasher worry she had just stepped over the line. "Sorry, I didn't mean to scare you."

Gently touching her hand, Kate said, "No, it's not that. I would love to meet your mother. I mean, you've had dinner with mine, right?"

"I think you know the difference." Dasher saw no reason to lie.

"I would be honored to meet your mother, Dash. But I don't want to frighten her. You said—"

"It'll be all right. She's a fan of yours. Besides, it's easier in a hospital setting. She knows there are lots of people around. I'm sure she'll be okay with it. I'll be there, which calms her. I'd like to introduce you two."

"Okay, let's go." Kate pulled her hand back and seemed suddenly shy. Dasher stood, almost dumping her scone on the ground, her face warming. What that was all about, she couldn't say.

They took the elevator, and as they entered the private room they heard quiet sniffling. Dasher's mother was lying in bed with her eyes closed, a beatific smile on her lips. She opened her deep brown eyes and held out her arms to Dasher, something so rare Dasher was momentarily at a loss. Then she walked over and gave her mother a hug, stealing a glance at Lupe, who wouldn't meet her gaze. She merely dabbed her face with a tissue and stared out the window.

"Mom, I brought someone to meet you. This is Kate—"

"Hoffman. Why, I'd know you anywhere. I really have enjoyed your movies, Miss Hoffman. Although I don't think they've tapped your abilities."

"Please call me Kate, and thank you. It's a pleasure to meet you, Mrs. Pate. Dasher…loves you so much."

Gazing fondly at Dasher, Mimi Pate said, "Oh, I know I've been a trial for poor Dasher. I couldn't ask for a better child, though. She has been such a bright light in my life. Are you two dating?"

Kate immediately glanced at the doorway and turned bright pink.

Dasher quickly said, "*Mom*, Kate and I are just friends. We ran into each other and I—"

"Just happened to want to introduce her to your shut-in mother, who you've never introduced to anyone before. I see." She was nodding at Lupe, who smiled wanly and still refused to look at Dash.

"Well, ah, I guess Kate should be going. I'll be right back, Mother." After all these years, her mother would pick today to get playful.

"But dear, you haven't heard the good news." Her mother seemed amused.

Glad to change the subject, Dasher said, "So, what is it?" It was unusual for her mother to have good news of any kind, let alone good news in a hospital.

"Well, I talked to the doctors." Dasher started to say something to Lupe, who was studying her lap, but her mother continued. "Now, don't be mad at Lupe. I asked her not to bother you."

"Well, I guess I wasn't needed, then. Clean bill of health, Mother?"

"Oh, no, my dear. I have cancer. I'm dying."

After that, Dasher only registered Kate taking her hand and Lupe crying. That and the fleeting thought that her mother's wish had finally been granted.

❖

Kate asked, "Where do I turn?"

They were on the Pacific Coast Highway, almost to Malibu. Dasher remembered Kate taking her keys and maneuvering her to the passenger side of the Cayenne. Then she informed her that she would drive her home so she could shower and change. Here they were.

"You didn't have to do this. What if someone sees you?" Dasher didn't mean the question sarcastically and hoped Kate understood that.

"So what? Joe's always complaining I don't get enough free publicity. Since I insist on wearing at least a thong and have never thrown a punch at anyone, this will have to do."

"Oh." Dash chose to drop the subject. What did she expect? For Kate to say that her friendship with Dasher was more important than her career? The fact that Kate cared enough to stay with her would have to do.

Kate's phone warbled. "Dasher, that's Laurel's ring. Would you answer? I don't know your car well enough to rummage through my purse for it. Don't want to end up in the ocean."

Seeing that Kate was only half joking, Dasher hurriedly pawed through a bunch of Kate's purse crap and found the phone. "Hi, Laurel. No, it's Dasher. Yes, this is Kate's phone. I'll let her explain." She smiled as she listened to Laurel sputter her surprise.

Kate held out her hand for the phone, eyes on the road, and hit the speaker button on the cell. "Hey, sis. What's up?"

"I think you might have found our new property up the coast, Kate."

"Really? Diana Tartaglia's property?" She shot a smile to Dasher, but try as she might, she couldn't return it. She could only replay the hospital scene and her mother's grand announcement.

"Didn't any others qualify?"

"Well, not all the results are in yet, but hers is practically turn-key, with lots of room to grow. She's offered it to the group for the weekend so we can check it out. We can't go up until after the opening, but we're excited."

"That's good news, then."

"Kate? Why's Dasher answering your phone? I don't mean to pry, but—"

"Okay, I'll talk to you later." She ended the call.

Dasher commented, "You aren't surprised she asked, are you?"

"No. I just didn't think now was a good time to get into it. Dash—she will ask again. What do you want me to say? You don't know Laurel, but she would never divulge any information. I've confided a million things and it stops there. Except, now that she's with Stef, I couldn't ask her to keep it from her. So, whatever you want, I'll do."

Dasher kept her eyes on the passing scenery. "I don't know Laurel, but I know Stef and I know you. You can tell her everything, but please ask them to keep it to themselves. Especially about…the last part."

Kate seemed pleased that Dasher trusted her with such personal information, but it appeared to make her anxious. She probably worried that Dasher might expect reciprocation because she abruptly changed the subject.

"Do you live right on the beach?"

"Well, technically I *rent* a tiny bungalow on the beach. So I guess the answer is yes."

"Good, let's take a stroll. I think we could both use some air."

Directed to a narrow driveway with broken cement and half-dead grass growing between the cracks, Kate drove past several homes and onto the sand-and-gravel drive that Dasher indicated.

Dasher took her keys from Kate and found the one for the house. She opened the screen door and keyed the lock, letting them in to a small tiled entryway with a tiny closet to the side. “Leave your shoes here. I have sandals you can wear. I’m going barefoot.” From the door there was a good view through the back slider of the ocean beyond.

It didn’t take long to walk through the cottage that Dasher always kept tidy. Kate glanced around, but if she was looking for photos, there weren’t any except in the bedroom.

When they reached the back deck Dasher opened the sliding door. “Take your pick.” She pointed to an array of sandals and flip-flops.

“Barefoot sounds perfect,” Kate said.

As exhilarating as the morning and beach were, Kate seemed more interested in watching Dasher.

She held out her hand. “Come on, sun’s a-wasting.”

The sound of the waves on the beach and the sight of California brown pelicans and white gulls swooping to catch a hapless fish or nab a sand crab for lunch soothed Dasher. Sandpipers used their beaks to drill for tiny treasures the waves washed up on shore, and their mad dashes here and there were comical to watch.

Southern California beaches were warm and sunny, the waves not as formidable as the ones up the coast. The air was clear and the breeze just right. The air in Malibu was quite different from the smog so often associated with Los Angeles proper.

There weren’t many people in sight yet, and those she

saw seemed intent on their own activities. The wet sand with the occasional tail end of a wave washing over their feet felt healing.

Kate linked her arm in Dasher's and they walked for a long time.

Finally, Dasher said, "She wants to die, you know. Has for years."

Probably trying to think of an appropriate platitude, Kate scowled into the sand for a moment, then sighed. "She did seem at peace about it."

Dasher scuffed her foot across a piece of seaweed bladder, and a small swarm of black insects flew away. "Yeah. And she insisted that you hear it, too. Why would she do that?"

"I'm not sure, but I think she wanted someone there for you. She sensed that we're friends. She knows I…care about you."

Dasher stopped, the breeze picking up her short hair and tossing it around. She gazed into Kate's eyes and for once Kate didn't look away.

"You care about me. You are my friend." As much as Dasher wanted it to be different between them, this was the truth of it, and she needed to accept that truth.

"Yes. It might sound trite to you, but I don't have many friends. I'd be honored if you would be mine." Her voice faltered for a moment, as if she was afraid she'd said too much.

Dasher's eyes dropped to Kate's lips and she was desperate for one more kiss. At that moment she didn't care if *People* magazine was shooting right beside them. But this was Kate, and if there could ever be more between them, it had to be Kate who came to her. If not, Dasher had to accept it or remove herself from Kate's life.

"Okay, friends it is. Thank you for being here, Kate. Thank you for being my friend." Dasher hoped she was convincing, but she knew she was a lousy liar.

Kate's expression seemed somewhere between relief and disappointment.

❖

When Kate walked in the door to her house the phone was ringing and she knew that Laurel was on the other end of the line. Feeling out of sorts, she snapped it to her ear. She was buzzing with so many emotions she couldn't name that Laurel was bound to pick up something. She wasn't ready for this conversation. "Hey, sis, what's up?"

"Nothing compared to what's up in Los Angeles, evidently. Let's hear it."

With a spontaneous, dramatic sigh Kate opened her heart to Laurel. Fifteen minutes later Laurel was still quiet. "Wow. That has to be pretty hard on Dasher. I'm glad you were there for her, hon. I'm proud of you."

Kate couldn't remember Laurel telling her she was proud of her for anything other than career-related things. Her words meant a lot. Maybe someday she'd have the courage to tell Laurel how much she craved her approval. Sadly, she realized that accepting compliments was easy for her. Giving them was another matter.

Laurel must have sensed Kate's discomfort, because suddenly they were talking about something else. "Hey, Jason Beresford is going to be in LA next week. He's too shy to ask, but he wondered if you wanted to go out to dinner or something. That was a quote. After you fairly dripped sexy all over him at the photo shoot, he's been a big fan."

"Oh, okay. Let me think. You know, I have to attend a

directors' dinner next Tuesday. If he wouldn't mind, it would save me having to dredge up an escort. At least he's nice and might have something to talk about other than himself. He'd need a tux."

Laughing, Laurel said, "He'll probably be gawking if a lot of celebrities are there. Hope you don't mind. He's a doll, the opposite of our own dear brother. And I'm sure he can dig up a tux."

"Sold. Give him my cell number, okay? Listen, I have to go. I have a meeting with Joe Alder in two hours and I'm a mess. Love you."

CHAPTER ELEVEN

Kate sat across from Joe and watched as he chewed his disgusting cigar and yapped on the phone. As much money as she made for him, how dare he treat her this way? She stood and folded her arms, glaring at him. He finally acknowledged her as if just noticing she was in the room.

"I gotta go. Call you later." After he flipped the phone onto his desk, he picked up a stack of what looked like manuscripts and tossed them across the desk. "Here, pick one and it's yours." He'd tried to give her disks in the past, but she insisted on a written script. She could get a better feel for the vehicle that way.

She sat and quickly thumbed through them. "Do any of them involve more than blowing things up and me half-naked?"

"Look, cupcake, you make us both a load of money doing those exploding naked things. What's to complain about? You can do the other shit once your tits head south. Now's the time to rake in the money." He looked quite satisfied with himself.

"Joe, I get your point, but there's no reason I can't establish myself as a serious actor before I'm playing someone's mother, and you know it." The way actors were referred to by their anatomy had always made her teeth hurt. She was, however, smart enough to know that her body played a part in her marketability. But she had established a name, and now she could try other roles.

His eyes narrowed. "You listening to that dyke bitch again?"

Her surprise must have been evident because he cackled. "Yeah, I know you've been seeing her. You think I'm stupid and can't figure out when someone's trying to poach? Listen, the only thing that woman wants is the commissions you'll bring in. Her clients don't make half what you do. Stay away from her."

"Some make less because their films are critical successes involving real acting. She has others that make more than me, according to *Variety*. And I haven't been *seeing* her, Joe. We happen to belong to the same charity and have worked on a committee together."

He rolled his eyes. "So that's why you two were snarfing down lattes when she was bailing that nut-job of a mother of hers out of the hospital—again. On the same committee."

The heat in her face was a blaze when she growled, "I saw her when I was leaving my physical therapy appointment for my knee, which happens to be located across from the hospital. Not that it's any of your business."

"Anything you do is my business." He started picking God-knows-what out of his fingernails and glared at her. "Just stay away, because if any rumors about you being a lezzie are going to hit the tabloids, I'm going to be in charge of them. And the bimbo will be a lot more famous than Dasher Pate."

Kate wanted out of there and stood abruptly. "You're disgusting."

He slammed his fist on the desk. "Don't think you can jump ship on our contract. I've got you signed up tighter than a drum until those gorgeous knockers of yours are sitting in your lap. Until *I* say so. Now read those scripts and pick one, *dear*."

Making a show out of checking his watch, he said, "If you'll excuse me, I have a lunch date with a really cooperative blonde who could replace you in a heartbeat."

Fuming, Kate picked up the stack, tempted to throw it at him. "Yeah, in a heartbeat. After only a few more rounds of surgery and a brain transplant. I still want a decent script."

He spat, "Sweetheart, the only way you'll get one of those is to write it yourself. And that would require some thinking and creativity on your part, now, wouldn't it? You've always been able to just show up and prance around. What makes you think you can do more?"

He was laughing as she stormed out of his office.

❖

Kate drove by the hospital without a real purpose. Spotting someone backing out of a parking spot, she pulled in, still without a plan. It wasn't until the automatic doors were opening that she was able to admit to herself that she was looking for Dasher.

Mrs. Pate's room was darker than usual, and Kate knocked lightly on the door, almost turning away because she didn't want to agitate the woman.

"Come in." It was certainly not Dasher's alto, but a higher version of the same voice.

Sticking her head in, Kate said, "Hi, Mrs. Pate. I was just in the neighborhood and thought I'd see if Dasher was here." *What a dumb idea. Dasher took the night shift.*

"Hello, Kate. Please come in. Lupe is just leaving to go get us some lunch. Would you like for her to get some for you, too?" She seemed rather cheerful, given the circumstances.

Lupe got up, smiled at her, and gathered her purse. "You stay here until I come back, okay?"

Feeling a bit trapped, Kate nodded, wondering what in hell she'd talk about. Mrs. Pate's impending death?

As Lupe hustled out the door, she said, "I bring back lots of chalupas."

Mimi Pate smiled at the closing door and said, "Oh dear, she loves chalupas. If you've never had the real deal, not the fast-food kind, you're in for a treat."

"I don't think I've had any kind of them. I don't know what they are."

"Lupe introduced them to me. They're pretty good. I think of them like small tostadas. Come, sit down. You look frazzled."

Somewhat surprised by the invitation, Kate sat.

"And call me Mimi. I'm not really Mrs. Pate anymore. The best thing I got from Jerry was Dasher. But I'm glad for his success. He loves his work."

Staring, Kate finally said, "Mrs.…Mimi, you are so—"

"Different than what you expected? I'm a little surprised, too. I guess knowing that I'm not here much longer has helped. You know, 'not my problem, got my orders,' that type of thing."

"Oh. Too bad you couldn't have done that sooner." The words were out before she could edit them. "I'm sorry, I didn't mean—"

"Yes, you did. I've wondered why Dash hasn't said something. I find you refreshing, Kate. You aren't at all like any of your publicity says."

Stung just a bit, Kate studied her. "I think I could say the same about you."

Smiling into her lap, Mimi said, "Now, you were looking for Dasher. Surely you have her cell number. What happened that you need her?"

Kate sighed. "I guess I just wanted someone to talk to. Dasher and I have agreed to be friends, and I needed a friend." She felt so pathetic.

"Agreed? Dasher is a good and true friend, if that's all you want. Why don't you try me out? I've never had many friends, either."

At that moment an understanding passed between them.

"Well, it's not much. Just agent problems. He thinks I'm only good for a paycheck and I want to actually act. Maybe I'm making it all up. Maybe he's right."

Suddenly quite serious, Mimi said, "Dasher believes you're a wonderful actor, and she knows a few things about talent. I happen to think you're wasted in those films, too. People are drawn to your beauty, yes, but there's more to you and they sense it."

"She does? You do?"

Her brown eyes held conviction when she said, "Yes. Dash and I agree on that subject."

"That really means a lot to me. Thank you." These two women were definitely not just complimenting her to get something from her. Or, if they were, she had no idea what it would be.

Lupe appeared at the door with several bags of food. They enjoyed the chalupas while discussing the joys of not eating in a hospital cafeteria more often than necessary.

As Lupe was cleaning up, Kate stood to excuse herself.

Mimi asked, "Where are you off to now, Kate?"

"Well, Joe saddled me with six scripts to go through. I'm going to my house to read them."

"You know, Lupe's desperate to clean my condominium for when I go home. Would you mind staying here to read them? We have at least one semi-comfortable chair you could use. I get nervous with strangers."

For the first time Kate saw for herself the fear that Dasher had described. How crippling to be so shy. She also felt honored to be included in the not-a-stranger category. She felt at ease with Mimi, too. So here she was again, doing something that wasn't her habit at all.

Kate glanced at Lupe and was met with a hopeful smile. "I don't see why not. I'll go get the manuscripts. But only if you'll read some of them, too, and tell me what you think. That could cut the time down by a lot."

"Wonderful. Dasher always has me read scripts for her. She says I can pick 'em."

Kate was delighted. Dasher's clients raved about her help in finding vehicles for them that challenged their skills. To have Mimi's advice would be a plus. The fact that Dasher would be there later, well, that was an added bonus.

After two hours passed they traded stacks. Kate asked, "Did you find one you liked?"

Mimi shook her head. "How many times can you make the same movie, Kate?"

Throwing her new stack onto the chair, she took the ones she'd just given to Mimi to toss on top. "That bastard. The truth is he'd rather substitute one of his cardboard blondes with fake everything. I'd bet their true talent is giving blow—er, sorry."

"Blow jobs? I may not like Hollywood, but I've certainly been around for a while. I agree with you. Can't you dump him and sign with Dasher?"

"Don't think I haven't thought about it. When I signed with him I was so young and stupid, he got me into a straightjacket of a contract. I don't think I could ever get out without him agreeing to release me. Besides, Dasher has never tried to poach, as Joe would so nicely put it. I doubt she's even interested."

Mimi was staring at the doorway. "Why don't you ask her?"

Kate whirled to see Dasher, a stunned look on her face, eyes dancing between the two of them.

"Mom? Kate?"

❖

Dasher was still in shock when Kate left an hour later, promising to return the next day so Lupe could have a break. Kate and her mother had chatted away like old friends. She'd never seen her mother become so friendly so quickly with another person.

"Dasher? You seem in another world. Is it Kate? She's lovely."

"Who are you and what have you done with my mother?"

Chuckling, Mimi said, "I guess I asked for that one. I don't know, but there's something about her I can't help but like. Maybe it's just the right circumstances. I suppose I don't have anything to be afraid of anymore. Or maybe it really is Kate. Are you sure you can't date her? I'd feel much better about leaving this earth if I knew you had someone."

"It's complicated." Dasher studied her new PDA. She'd just bought it and was planning to set it up during her time with her mother. They usually didn't talk much, but that seemed to have changed. Kate had groused because her mother was always trying to fix her up. Now Dasher's mother was taking an interest. Was this a "mom" thing?

"Her agent sounds awful. What do you think of him?"

"He's lower than pond scum, and I'd rather have Kate with almost anyone but him."

"So, you'd like to have her as a client, then."

"You could say that." Dasher was trying to be vague but evidently failing.

"I knew it. You're in love with her."

Reaching the point of exasperation, Dasher said, "Mom! This isn't…I can't… Kate and I are friends. She's straight and I'm not. See the difference there?"

Looking perplexed, Mimi countered. "What I see, young lady, is a lonely woman who gets by on bravado and beauty and needs a friend. I never had her bravado, but for a while there I was sought after, and I understand her need. I've also seen the way she looks at you. Dash, have you ever been in love?"

The suddenly feisty Mimi Pate looked determined to get an answer. The truth popped out of Dasher's mouth without her permission. "Yes, five years ago."

After a moment, Mimi said, "I remember. You were so excited about signing a new actress. Then a month later you never mentioned another word about her. I noticed, Dasher, despite what you might think. What was her name?"

Giving up the charade, Dash admitted the truth. "Kate Hoffman."

"Oh, Dash. I'm sorry. Maybe this time things will be different."

"Mom, I'm not holding my breath. Some things just aren't meant to be."

Nodding, she said, "And some things are fated to be. No matter how hard you try, you can't outrun them. Don't give up on her, Dash. Maybe she just has to find her way to you."

Dasher grumbled, "I'm still wondering what you did with my mother." But she was enjoying listening to her. What she didn't say was that dying seemed to agree with Mimi Pate.

"Tell you what, let's watch a Western. We both love horses."

Dasher put her new PDA in her pocket for another time

and dug through a box of DVDs she'd brought from her mother's place. Although Dash had a few childhood memories of camping, she never could figure out why Mimi liked cowboy films so much. From what little her mother would say, she'd been raised poor and in a city. Rolling tundra seemed like an odd thing for an agoraphobic to long for.

❖

The next day Kate and Mimi were watching an early Clint Eastwood Italian Western and laughing at the acting and dialogue when Dasher came unexpectedly early. Kate was delighted until she saw Dasher's face.

"What's wrong?" She looked ready to tear something in two.

Mimi regarded Dasher. "Oh. You must've talked to my doctors."

"Yeah, I have. Do you want to know what they told me?"

Kate hit the Stop button on the DVD player. From the expression on both women's faces, this didn't involve her.

Mimi said, "Now, Dasher—"

As if she'd been struck, Dasher flinched. "Don't you dare 'Now, Dasher' me, Mom. Don't you dare."

"I should go." Kate started to rise and Dasher held up her hand.

"No. Stay. You can hear this. Mother, would you like to give the bad news to Kate?"

Mimi was silent, staring at the dark screen on the DVD player.

"Dash…"

Kate didn't have any idea what to do.

Dasher ignored her. "Seems my mother has cancer, yes,

but it's probably quite treatable. They would have to do surgery to remove a tumor in her uterus and then go from there, depending on what they find."

"Well, that's wonderful, right?" Why did Dasher look so anguished?

"I've refused the surgery," Mimi said. "Does that about sum it up, sweetie?"

"Yes. You're so happy to be dying that no one or nothing can spoil your fun, especially not the prospect of actually living. Because why would you want to do that? No one cares about you, no one *loves* you. No one that matters anyway."

"Dash!" Kate exclaimed.

Mimi touched Kate's arm and said, "No, let her talk."

"You know, Mother, I have power of attorney for legal and health matters. I could have you declared incompetent and force you to get that surgery." The anger and pain that were so evident in Dasher's eyes broke Kate's heart.

Regarding her evenly, Mimi said, "But you won't."

The standoff lasted maybe ten seconds, then Dasher dropped her head, the fire replaced by resignation. The next time she met her mother's gaze she said, "No. If there's nothing here worth living for, I can't do a damned thing about it." She turned and left the room.

The gravity of what had just happened and what Dasher had said hit Kate like a punch in the chest. She whirled on Mimi. "How could you do that?"

Shaking her head, Mimi said, "The odd thing is, I've been thinking about having the surgery, trying to see if I can do better this time, and it was all for Dasher. But I can't guarantee that anything will change. Don't you think I've caused enough pain to that lovely woman? Don't you think it's best for Dasher?"

"What are you talking about?"

"I'm saying that Dasher could live her life if she didn't have the albatross named Mimi hanging around her neck." Her eyes were shimmering with tears.

Kate walked over to her, took both her shoulders, and looked her in the eye. "You just told Dasher that she wasn't important enough to even keep you alive. You confirmed her worst fears about herself. This isn't about you any longer, Mimi. It's time for you to be her mother. Excuse me."

When she stormed out the door, she heard quiet sobbing behind her.

❖

Kate couldn't find Dasher anywhere. She tried the garden, looked in the waiting rooms on every floor, even got caught for a few autographs while scanning the cafeteria. Finally she happened upon the chapel. When she entered she saw only one person. Dasher was sitting quietly in a pew, staring at the wall that contained representations of several of the world's religions: a cross, a Star of David, a statue of a sitting Buddha, and the crescent moon and five-pointed star to represent Islam. Rows of votive candles were available for people to light to pray for their loved ones, and the faint odor of incense filled the air. The place was quiet and peaceful.

Kate sat beside Dasher, took her hand and squeezed it, then clasped their hands together in her lap. Dasher's strong profile revealed tear tracks the length of her face, but her eyes were dry.

"Why are you still here?" Dasher asked. "I would think you'd have run screaming from this place a long time ago." The roughness of her voice confirmed that she'd been crying.

"I've been looking for you. I was afraid you'd done the same thing."

"Nah. I'll get it together and go back. She'll be frightened."

Kate turned away from the religious icons and faced Dasher. "Look at me, Dash, please."

Finally, Dasher met her eyes and Kate confirmed what she feared. She saw shame. "If your mother chooses not to have the surgery, that's on her. You are one of the most loving, compassionate human beings I've ever known. I could never be one-tenth the person you are. Just knowing you are my friend makes me a better person." Kate realized that she could have sold this as a dramatic scene, but she meant every word.

She kissed Dasher's forehead and then her cheek, slightly grazing the corner of her mouth. "I am in awe of you."

They held each other's gaze until someone came in the room. The spell broken, they walked out together.

Just as they opened the door a man cleared his throat and they looked up to see Chaz Hockaday busily shooting photos, his face still covered in scratches and blisters. His partner in crime, Michael, was standing to the side, looking as though he wished he were anywhere but there. He waved and smiled apologetically.

Dasher was taken aback, then stepped in front of Kate. "Hockaday, can't you leave Miss Hoffman alone?"

Kate was surprised, then pleased that her knight was trying to protect her.

"Aw, come on, you know how it is. Catching the two of you together is putting food on my table. Now, be a sport and move so I can get a few more."

He was grinning and started shooting again when Kate stepped out from behind Dasher.

Kate smiled slyly. "I see you're looking better today. Tell me, were your face and arms the only places you got the sap? I know it's hard to wash off."

One of his hands dropped toward his crotch, but he caught himself and she could swear that underneath all those sores was a blush. She nodded thoughtfully. "Yes, I was afraid of that. I'll bet it itches constantly, no matter what you put on it, right? You want to scratch, but then it spreads and gets worse. Just itching and itching."

"Hey, shut up! It doesn't itch that much." He looked uncomfortable even saying the word.

"You don't sound very convincing. My brother got it on his penis once and it drove him crazy. Itching and itching, so tender. Of course, he couldn't have sex, but all that scratching and then it was painful when he'd, well, you know. He got oozing sores."

The horror on both men's faces was a sight to see. Chaz growled, "Bitch," then took off for, presumably, the bathroom. Michael was right behind him.

Snorting, Dasher said, "You are evil. That poor man may never recover."

"Serves him right. Food on the table, my ass."

"I hope he doesn't cause you any problems."

"He probably will. Listen, I have to run. Are you going to the directors' dinner Tuesday night? I have to show up."

"Me, too. Do you want to go together?" Dasher seemed to suddenly realize what she'd asked and looked away awkwardly.

"I'm sorry, Dash, I can't. I invited Jason Beresford because he plans to be in town. He's kind of my brother-in-law and I thought it would be nice...you know." She wanted to apologize but Dasher immediately shut down further discussion.

"No problem. I'll probably take Greta. She still loves all the awards stuff, and it's good for her to be seen. She's not dating anyone, so she'll be up for it. Besides, Joe would probably follow through with his threat to call security."

"So, I'll see you there. Tuesday." Kate wondered when Joe had made such a threat, but Dasher disappeared before she could ask.

When Dasher had mentioned inviting Greta, Kate used all her willpower to bite back a remark about probably still seeing things through a child's eyes. She was jealous and had no right, no right at all. After all, she was taking Jason to the event. They had agreed, at Kate's insistence, that they were only friends. Her reasoning didn't help the gnawing in her gut that the idea of Dasher with Greta created.

Chapter Twelve

Dasher had the limo wait while she walked to the door to collect Greta. The rental house that she'd helped Greta lease when she first arrived in Los Angeles had worked perfectly. Its courtyard with a high-end security system in place so she could see who was ringing the bell was especially useful.

Greta answered the front door with an enthusiasm Dasher certainly didn't share, but she tried to not spoil the prospect of the high-profile dinner for her.

"Hi, Dash! Are you ready for the rubber chicken?" Greta got a huge kick out of referring to these events that way. She also loved to tease Dasher about her tendency to avoid them when possible. Her slight Russian accent matched her classic pale features and the slim build of a ballerina.

Dasher had seen her in a small independent film two years before and signed her immediately. In Greta she'd found a hardworking, vibrant woman who appreciated everything to its maximum.

But even Greta's positive personality couldn't make up for the fact that, yet again, Dasher would have to try to avoid coming in contact with Kate. It hurt worse this time, too. Odd, she didn't think that was possible, but it was.

Dasher and Greta wove their way through the crowd, looking for their nameplates on the many round tables set with golden flatware, fine china, and elegant floral centerpieces. Both spent time waving to colleagues or acquaintances, and Greta finally found their table.

Feeling like a soldier on a forced march, Dasher couldn't help but scan the room nervously for Kate and Jason. She was relieved that they hadn't yet shown up, but the anticipation made her conversational skills, already sketchy in crowds, absent.

Greta spoke near Dasher's ear, competing with the crowd noise. "Hey, Dasher, are you ill? You don't look so good."

"Oh, I'm fine. You know how much I like these things." Her halfhearted laugh didn't seem to fool Greta.

"I see. Oh, look, there's Kate Hoffman and that handsome man I saw when we went to the hotel a few weeks ago. He's so cute!"

Grabbing a glass of champagne someone had placed in front of her, Dasher took a gulp and stared at the stage where the awards would be presented.

"Dasher? I said…" Then Greta fell silent. A few seconds passed before she continued. "I see. Well, we must do something about this. I'll be back."

Not caring what Greta was babbling about and relieved to have a moment to herself, Dasher drained the champagne glass and eyed Greta's. There was a lot of activity around their table as people arrived. The sound of clothing rustling as a woman took her seat beside Dasher brought her out of her state, and she gutted up to make small talk.

Turning, she became lost in a sea of apple green and a most beautiful smile. Kate Hoffman sat right beside her.

"Hi, Dasher. Fancy meeting you here."

She wore a curve-hugging strapless gown that made her

look like a goddess. While most were lusting for Kate's body, and Dasher certainly worshipped it, too, she couldn't pull herself from those eyes that held something just for Dasher in them. The weight that forced her inertia was suddenly lifted, dissolved. Another form of heaviness replaced it, one that settled farther south.

"Hey, Dasher, isn't this great?" Jason was bending down to kiss her cheek. She felt like she was in a dream. She turned to Greta, who was grinning mischievously.

"You did this."

"I did. I saw their names on another table and did a switch." Tapping her temple with her forefinger she narrowed her eyes and said, "You look much better now. See? Trust Greta."

Swiveling back to Kate, Dasher managed only, "You're here."

Kate's lovely mouth opened a full five seconds before she whispered, "Yes." The word had so much more meaning in it than the fact she had arrived at the event.

Only vaguely aware of her surroundings, Dasher heard Greta introduce herself to Jason and saw Kate blink, then seem to tune in to the room.

Kate said, "Oh, I'm sorry. Jason, this is Greta Sarnoff. Greta, meet Jason Beresford."

Never taking her gaze from Jason, Greta said, "I have wanted to meet this man since I first saw him." She held out her hand palm down, a very European greeting.

Dasher recognized enchantment when she saw it. Jason took her hand and gallantly bowed and kissed the back of it. Judging from Greta's smile, that was the perfect response.

"Kate, would you mind if Jason sits beside me until our other table guests join us?" Greta was quite the organizer.

Kate tried to make herself heard. "Knock yourself out." The room noise was picking up.

Greta looked momentarily shocked until Dasher said, "That means 'yes,' Greta."

She seemed delighted as she settled Jason next to her.

"Dasher, I'm pretty sure I wasn't seated at your table," Kate said. "In fact, when Joe Alder gets here he'll probably blow an artery."

"Couldn't happen to a nicer fella. Much as I'd like to take credit, we'll have to blame Greta. She switched the place cards."

"I'm beginning to think I misjudged Miss Sarnoff."

"Maybe she just wanted to steal your date. I'm sure that's what the tabloids will say tomorrow."

Glancing in Jason's direction, Kate said, "He's probably in heaven. I wasn't much company."

Dasher's heart rate rose another notch. "I wasn't either. I think Greta figured that out."

"I've definitely misjudged her. Maybe I should send flowers."

"No, I'll take care of that."

Greta tapped Dasher on the back, looking perturbed. "Who is that red-faced man glaring at us?" She pointedly stared over Dasher's shoulder.

Joe Alder had arrived at his table and was now glaring death rays at Dasher.

"This could get ugly," Dasher said.

Jason stood, saying, "I'll explain everything."

Then Greta pulled on his sleeve. "No, let me. I speak his language." She left them all sitting at the table, staring after her.

For a good five minutes, until the lights started to dim, signaling the event was beginning, they talked. At first Alder made jabbing gestures toward Kate and Dasher. Then he settled down and was listening, and finally he nodded slyly, like he agreed with everything she said. The entire time his eyes roamed over Greta's generous cleavage and her body. He made Dasher queasy.

Greta returned to the table and sat, downing the champagne in front of her in one gulp. They all bent forward to hear what had happened.

"That man is disgusting. He talked to my boobies the whole time. Kate, you must get away from him, he's not good for you."

Kate nodded. "I wish I could. What did you say to him? Why didn't he drag me back to his table?"

Smiling, Greta said, "I told him I have arranged a publicity stunting. I pretend to try to steal Jason from you and you get angry. You and I have to have a pussy battle when this is over. Okay?"

After a full beat of silence, Kate started laughing. Grinning at them, especially Dasher, Kate said, "I'd love it. But I think it's called a catfight. At least I hope so."

❖

In the limo on the way back to Greta's house, Dasher said, "Well, that was quite a pus…er, catfight. Front page on the tabloids, I'll bet. You two are very good actors, do you know that?"

Dasher was still savoring the fact that she'd sat next to Kate all evening, their thighs welded together under the drape of the tablecloth. At intervals she'd chance a sideways glance at Kate and always caught a grin coming from her. When she could tear herself away from Kate and turned her attention to Greta, Jason and she were deep in conversation. The other couples at their table had simply worked around their seating arrangement.

At one point, Kate draped an arm over the back of Dasher's chair and reached across Dash to speak to Greta. Her dress left little to the imagination anyway, and at this angle… Dasher glued her eyes to Jason's, well aware they were both trying their best to be polite. They were probably the only two doing so.

Kate told Greta she loved her dress, but her face looked tense and angry. Greta responded with much thanks and a return of the compliment, but her body and face telegraphed, "Belligerent." Amazing.

When they stood to leave, Kate politely gave Dasher a hug, whispering in her ear, "See you at the hospital." She then possessively held on to Jason and dragged him out of the room. Once outside where the paparazzi wielded even more cameras, Kate and Greta seemed furious with each other and huffed off in different directions, Dasher and Jason trailing after their respective dates. The scene was a masterpiece.

Greta looked pleased. "That was fun. And I have a date with Jason. I think he might be special."

"Really? That's great. Yeah, he's a very nice guy. His sister, Stefanie, is a good friend. That's how I got the invitation to the hotel. She and her partner, Laurel, own it."

"Oh, *that's* what Jason was talking about. I wasn't at the hotel that long when I went with you. Laurel is Kate's sister, right? I intended to ask. So, how was your evening, Ms. Pate?" Her grin was infectious.

Smiling and probably blushing, too, Dasher said, "The best rubber chicken I've ever eaten. Thank you, Greta."

Shaking her head, Greta said, "No, I thank you. When you signed me to a contract I was almost out of money and luck. Believe me, that awful man tonight is nothing compared to some of the men I've had to deal with." The momentary sadness in her eyes caught Dash off guard.

Not knowing what to say, Dasher took her hand. "I guess we're friends, then. He would have made a scene if you hadn't thought up that stunt."

Greta sighed. "Kate really cares for you. She must be afraid."

"Yeah, her branding is all about appealing to young boys and men. She's straight, anyway, so it doesn't matter."

"Straight? Piffle. It is about one heart connecting to another heart. Once you realize that, the rest is simple."

Dasher nodded. *Piffle?* She'd come to that conclusion five years ago. But the truth that followed her like a specter was that both hearts had to believe. If one didn't, the other couldn't force it. She'd learned that from her mother. Evidently she hadn't learned it well enough.

"Well, sometimes you just have to be grateful for a special rubber-chicken dinner."

Flopping against the seat and staring ahead, Greta squeezed her hand and sighed tiredly. *"Da."*

After seeing Greta to her door, Dasher dozed in the back of the limousine. Long ago she had learned to live in the moment. Wishing and hoping had only brought heartache. As of *this* moment she had a friend in Greta, and Kate had told her she'd see her tomorrow. Dasher took a risk and looked forward to that possibility.

CHAPTER THIRTEEN

Dasher stopped by Mimi's condo to grab a suitcase early the next morning. She didn't need to stay at the hospital any longer. Dasher mentally forced herself not to anticipate what the next few months or years would bring. After all, live in the moment, right? She could handle it.

After surreptitiously checking to see that Kate wasn't in the garden, she started mentally making lists of chores for Lupe and herself. Lists always helped her when things were spinning out of control. When she entered her mother's room, she was surprised to see her mother's physician and several nurses, busily attaching things and having her sign forms.

Kate stood by quietly and looked thrilled to see Dasher. Momentarily caught in Kate's gaze, Dash eventually realized that her mother was talking to her.

"Oh, good, you're here. Would you all excuse us? Not you, Kate. Please stay."

Kate nodded, standing a few feet from the bed as the others cleared away. Her hands were behind her back and she was fidgeting. She looked like a fourteen-year-old schoolgirl with a secret she was dying to tell. God, she was beautiful.

"What are you two up to?" Dasher tried to ignore a feeling of being left out of the pack. How was it that Kate could march in and be instant friends with Dasher's mother? The unusual and unexpected turn of events made her feel happy and a bit envious at the same time.

"Dasher, do you mind if I have the surgery?" From the expression on her mother's face and in her eyes, she wasn't joking. She was actually asking permission.

"Why are you asking me? Don't you think I'd want you to? Oh." When she realized what was behind the question, she gasped.

Incredulous, she turned to Kate for verification and saw it in her eyes. They were both waiting for her decision. Anger was the only emotion that surfaced.

"What happens then, Mom? What if the surgery is a success and you get better, just to go back to being miserable? Is that my fault? What happens if you need more chemo or radiation? Is that when you quit? Am I responsible for that?"

Kate saw the anguish in Dasher's face and ached to be next to her, to hold her hand. To protect her. She stayed where she was. Whatever happened next was between mother and daughter.

Mimi said, "No! Yes...but it's not your responsibility, Dasher. It never has been. I just don't want to put you through any more. I'm terrified that I'll have a second chance and *I'll* fail *you*."

Kate couldn't stop herself. She went to Dasher's side and slipped an arm around her waist. "Mimi, if you take this chance, won't the rest seem easy? I mean, this is the risk to live. This decision says you're ready to change."

The air in the room was charged in their collective silence. A nurse dressed in blue scrubs bustled in and stopped, taking them all in. "Have you signed the form, Mrs. Pate?"

Looking directly into Dasher's eyes, Mimi smiled and handed her the clipboard. "Yes, here it is."

The woman checked it over and said, "Okay, surgery is scheduled for seven o'clock. The anesthesiologist will be in very early tomorrow. See you in there."

"You've already signed it?" Dasher's voice was just above a whisper.

"Yes. I want your support, Dasher, but I'm doing this. I want to try. If I fail, then nothing has changed. Kate said it well. As I thought about it, somehow I realized that's no longer an option. I've already changed. Perhaps the opportunity to die made me realize how precious life is and how I'd been wasting that opportunity. I want to be your mother…again. I hope you'll let me have that chance."

Kate and Dasher sat in the garden in silence. Kate was tired. This friendship business was tricky. She hoped Eleanor Roosevelt was happy. She ventured a question. "Are you okay?"

"Thank you. Your friendship with Mom seems to have made a real difference to her." Kate detected a tone of she wasn't sure what.

"What do you mean?" Somehow this conversation felt more dangerous than the one that had just transpired in the hospital room.

"I mean, hell, I mean I've been trying to get my mother to change my whole life. A few days with you and bingo, she's a new woman."

"What? Dasher, that's not true. Your mother has…is ill. It's a life-threatening situation. That was the catalyst. I happened to be there and she doesn't have any history with me. It could have been Lupe or a nurse or someone else." Why did she feel defensive?

Without rancor, Dasher shook her head. "I think you're right, but I also think it was you, not anyone else. You have a special touch with her. So, thank you."

Kate let out a long, slow breath. "Phew. I was afraid you hated me."

A look of confusion crossed Dasher's features. "I could never hate you. Be frustrated, irritated, confused, flabbergasted—"

Holding up a hand, Kate said, "Okay, okay, I get it. So, are we friends?" Somehow Dasher's response meant so much.

Dasher held up her pinkie finger. "Pinkie swear."

Kate stared at the offer of a childhood promise. Her first one. They joined pinkies, and in that moment, Kate realized that their bond was as deep as innocence itself.

She also realized something else. For all of their friendship promises, she knew she was lying, lying to her friend. Most of all, she was lying to herself.

She liked some people a great deal, she kept in touch with others, and some she just enjoyed talking to. She had Laurel to confide in, but she'd never met someone, male or female, who she constantly wanted to touch, to be with, to make happy.

When Dasher offered her pinkie and Kate accepted it, her life changed. Kate absently wondered if she could take it back, but, like Mimi and her choice to have the surgery, the genie was out of the bottle. Kate Hoffman had never felt this way about anyone before. It was terrifying and wonderful, all at once. She pictured Eleanor Roosevelt laughing and clapping her hands. That woman had a weird sense of humor.

❖

Kate, Dasher, and Lupe sat together in the waiting room reserved for families of those having surgery. Other groups of loved ones were there passing the time while their special person was undergoing a procedure, and Kate could tell a few recognized her. They tried to give her privacy, but they were clearly watching. After all, it was a distraction from the tedium and fear. Dasher paced, made phone calls, and worried her PDA. Lupe knitted, and Kate worked on her laptop.

At one point, Chaz Hockaday appeared, took one photo, and looked about to shoot more. Honestly, that man. Kate noticed he didn't look so blotchy and his buddy Michael wasn't with him. She hoped he'd found something better to do.

Dasher was in no shape to take him on, but she visibly tensed and got ready to do battle with him in spite of being preoccupied with her mother's surgery. Kate had put her hand on Dasher's forearm to signal she would handle Chaz when he suddenly stilled, stared over their heads, then slipped out of the door that led to the stairs. Confused, they both turned and saw a formidable-looking man with steel gray hair and Dasher's eyes. She'd never met Jerry Pate but thought that was about to change.

"Dad, what are you doing here?" Dasher's confusion seemed genuine.

He ambled to the chair on the other side of Dash and sat. In a voice obviously meant just for her, he said, "Did you think I wouldn't come? Mimi is still my wife and you're my daughter. Have you heard anything?"

He glanced cursorily at Kate but kept his focus on Dasher. Kate thought she detected concern and love in his eyes. For all of their estrangement, they were a family, and Kate felt a sense of relief for Dasher.

"No, not yet. She's been in surgery for two hours."

"Why the photog? What was he doing here?" The question seemed more directed at Kate and she realized that was his intent. He probably thought she'd arranged it.

Feeling guilty, Kate said, "I should have stayed away. That man has been following me for weeks. If I wasn't here, you could have had your privacy. I apologize, Dasher. I just thought you shouldn't be alone." She shot an accusing glare at Dasher's father, who had the decency to look away. She refused to back down to this man.

Dasher regarded her father and said, "Dad, this is Kate Hoffman. Kate has been a regular visitor lately. She and Mom are friends. Please don't run her off."

He grinned. "Okay, okay, sorry." He extended his hand to Kate. "I'm Jerry. And, of course, I know who you are. My crew argued with Joe Alder until we were hoarse to get you to not try that particular stunt. That guy is an asshole, no offense."

Kate shook her head, appreciating his candor. "None taken. I learned the hard way that stunts should be left to the professionals. I thought your crew was excellent, but I just wasn't up to the task. I'll leave it to you from now on, no matter what Joe says."

Jerry glanced between the two and asked, "You're friends with Dash and Mimi? How did that happen? I thought you blew her off a long time ago."

"Dad! Please, let's try for diplomacy, okay?" Dasher was turning a bright pink, and Kate knew her own fair complexion didn't hide anything, either.

Each one of them glanced around to see who might be listening. This town had eyes and ears everywhere. The one couple still in the room was in a deep discussion with a doctor. Judging from Lupe's curt nod and watchful expression, she had been keeping an eye on things. Kate liked her more each time they met.

"Mr. Pate—Jerry, Dasher and I reconnected through a mutual friend and we belong to the same, er, charity. And yes, I did sign with Joe instead of Dasher." She kept her gaze even with his. "It was a mistake."

Lupe's knitting needles clacked faster, probably to keep her from nodding in agreement.

Dasher looked down, her blush deepening. Then Jerry Pate cleared his throat, which was the only reason Kate remembered he was there.

"Why don't you dump that guy and sign with Dash?"

Dasher's head jerked up and she rolled her eyes. "Dad! You're starting to sound like Mom. Stop, please."

He folded his massive arms across his equally massive chest. "Your mother is a very smart woman. Just because we've gone our separate ways doesn't mean I don't appreciate her. When she's not drinking, she's the best."

Kate thought she saw regret in his expression. She could relate. Both of them absented themselves from their problems by working. That didn't mean the problems went away. They usually just got worse.

The door opened then and the surgeon who had spoken with Dasher before came bustling in. They all stood as she approached.

"Ms. Pate?" She looked askance at the rest of them.

"It's okay. This is my dad and the rest are dear friends. We can all hear. How is she?"

"We did a complete hysterectomy. The tumor is removed, and there didn't appear to be any others in the abdominal cavity. We took some tissue samples to check microscopically, but as of now, we've done what we can surgically. You'll need to talk to the oncologist about the next steps." Glancing at her watch, she said, "She'll be in recovery for the next few hours, then moved back to her room. Barring any complications, you can see her then. She'll be out of it until tomorrow. I suggest getting something to eat, all of you."

The collective sigh of relief was audible. After each of them, including Lupe, shook the surgeon's hand, she strode out of the waiting room, leaving them alone.

Jerry shoved his hands in the back pockets of his designer jeans and studied the ceiling. "Well, uh, can I buy all of you ladies lunch? I'd like to at least say hello to Mimi when she wakes up. Of course, I understand if you have other plans."

Lupe shyly shook her head. "I go home and come back. I must see to my granddaughter when she comes from school."

Kate let Dasher decide. She might want to spend time alone with her father. Dasher briefly gave Kate a look that she understood immediately. Dasher wanted her to stay. Kate agreed with only her eyes. How odd that they'd known each other only a few weeks, not counting the five years before, and they were communicating without words like a couple. Like she'd seen her parents do. She had read about things like that.

Dasher turned to her father, who had been watching intently, and Kate was sure he hadn't missed a thing. His expression was unreadable, but he seemed pleased when they both agreed.

❖

Kate left the hospital at eight o'clock and drove straight home. If she'd been tired before, she was exhausted now. Mimi was rather groggy, but she had squeezed Kate's hand and thanked her for being there for her and Dash. She seemed happy to hear Jerry's voice, and they were holding hands when Kate and Dasher slipped out of the room.

Holding hands. She had so wanted to hold Dasher's hand in the waiting room, but hadn't. She'd wanted to take her hand again in the hallways, the elevator, at the restaurant. But she didn't.

She'd held hands with some of her dates, her sister, her mother. She'd seen girls do it in high school and college, but she had so few female friends, it seemed foreign to her.

Now she was obsessing about what holding Dasher's hand would be like. She knew she couldn't. Look what happened every time they touched! It would be like kissing her, for God's sake. Kissing would be next, she had no doubt. Probably more, and that thought overheated every system in her body.

If she held Dasher Pate's hand she'd never stop and her career would be over. Teenage boys and young men were so homophobic, they'd drop her at the box office immediately. Her gay male actor friends told her that was why they needed to keep their orientation a secret—straight women didn't like their fantasies exploded. The movies were a business of illusion, after all.

She couldn't worry about that right now. The larger problem was *why* she wanted to hold Dasher's hand. Could she really be falling in love with her? Would that make her a lesbian like Laurel? Well, *yeah*.

It would also answer some questions that had been popping into her head lately. Like, why was she so content to help her gay friends out if they needed a date? Answer: She needed one, too. One that ended with a chaste good-night peck on the cheek or sleeping in a separate bedroom. The tabloids billed her as wanton and lusty, which was nowhere near the truth. Except when she thought of Dasher.

Next question: Why did she go out only with straight men who were jerks, more interested in publicity than in her, and she could easily dump? Answer: She just wasn't drawn to men who were straight, decent, and obviously attracted to her. Like Jason Beresford. Although after seeing him with Greta, she had revised that thought. Jason might have been attracted to Kate, yet he was entranced with Greta. But there were others. Her mother kept telling her she was too picky. She kept telling herself that she just hadn't met the right one. Was that true?

Or was the truth that she *had* met the right one, five years ago? The ramifications of that possibility were so complex that Kate had to sit down. Then she stood up, poured a glass of Syrah, and sat down again. Then she went to her home gym and worked out, showered, tried to eat something, and sat down once more in front of the untouched glass of wine.

How would she explain this new development to her parents? Her fans? Her staff? Like it or not, celebrities were cottage industries. They employed publicists, agents, attorneys, assistants, drivers, and the list went on. She risked her career and disappointing so many.

Warning herself not to leap to conclusions, she tried for some perspective. Kate knew without a doubt that she was drawn to Dasher. But maybe she was simply bored and loved drama. She was between projects, around all those lesbian friends of Laurel and Stefanie.

She stared at the wine. She really liked those women but didn't want to date them. Just hang out. They were real. They treated her like a friend. This was a new environment and she liked it. That was it. She didn't want to date one of them, although a few were pretty hot.

She sorted through the mail and stopped when she arrived at a large manila envelope hand-addressed to her from Laurel. Few people had her personal street address.

She opened it and saw the proof sheets from the photo shoot. She was musing that the photographer had done a good job when she skidded to a halt at the shots of her and Dasher on that huge motorcycle. There it was—all the confirmation she needed.

She sipped. Dasher, those damned eyes. They had somehow burned into her soul the moment Kate met her. If she was being completely honest, with herself at least, she conjured them up when she was performing a love scene in a film. And when she couldn't fall asleep at night. Dasher's eyes held mystery and a deep understanding that she'd never found before or since, and that lulled her into a complete sense of serenity.

She'd always reasoned that it was her imagination, but getting to know Dasher only confirmed her fantasy. Oh, God. Things had changed, because now when she envisioned Dasher's eyes, she wasn't able to fall asleep at all. Rather, she became aroused to the point of no sleep. And she didn't see much rest in her future, either, because she was getting worse.

The moment Dasher had touched her at the hotel photo shoot, her carefully constructed papier-mâché life had begun to dissolve and she didn't see how she could paste it back together. As she gazed at the pictures, the proof was right in front of her.

Draining her glass, she choked on the last drops. It hadn't occurred to her until that moment that there was one more risk in this whole scenario. Perhaps it was the biggest one. What if Dasher didn't feel the same way?

Why would she care what Kate was feeling after the shabby way Kate had treated her for the past five years? She'd be crazy to have anything but resentment toward her. The thought of Dasher turning her back on Kate made her stomach twist painfully.

She carefully washed the crystal wineglass, dried it, and put it in the cabinet. Walking purposefully to her home office, she methodically opened the computer and checked her calendar. By rearranging some magazine interviews and doing one by telephone, she could put a few days together. Laurel had asked her if she'd do a final run-through of the hotel opening that was less than two weeks away.

She made her reservations.

CHAPTER FOURTEEN

Dasher sat in the garden in the hospital and sipped her coffee, leaving the scone untouched. Each day she waited for Kate, and each day her disappointment tore at her heart just a bit more.

It had been four days since Dasher returned from dinner with her father and tried to call Kate, only to have the call roll to voice mail. She must have pressed that number twenty times but stopped leaving messages after the first day. After three days she stopped herself from even calling, trying to salvage some dignity. Kate knew how to find her.

Her father had confronted her about her feelings for Kate and warned her that this might happen.

"Kate, honey, for all the world knows, she's straight. I haven't even heard rumors to the contrary, and you know how this town talks. Has she given you any encouragement? Have you slept with her?"

Knowing she was probably blushing furiously, she had blurted, "Dad! No, but…we kissed once." She was painfully aware of how pathetic that sounded.

Her dad scrubbed his face as if trying to contain himself. "Dasher, that's not much to base your love on. She's a star, and her demographic won't tolerate her being in a lesbian relationship. Unless you want to add a boy and make it a three-way."

She couldn't believe his comment. "No! No way. Oh, God." Could this be any more awful?

They didn't speak while he paid for their meal. "Honey, why don't you talk to your mom about this? I'm obviously not very good at comforting you. I just don't want you to get hurt, that's all. But if you ever need someone's ass kicked, I'll be there."

He'd waited with her until the valet brought her car around. Kissing her forehead, he said, "If it helps, she won't be a teenage hard-on much longer. But I'd sure find out how she feels about you. Take care, and give my love to your mom. I'll be up to visit in a few days."

Dasher knew her dad loved both her mom and her. He just was a little ham-handed around emotions. And his attempts to express them, well, they were honest, at least.

Her mother had asked for Kate not long after the surgery, and when Dasher told her she wasn't answering her calls, Mimi took her hand and held it for a long time. Still a bit sleepy from the anesthesia, Mimi seemed clear-headed when she said, "Give her time, sweetie, give her time."

"Time. Now there's a concept." Dasher shook off the thought and rose from the bench, knowing she wouldn't see Kate today. The weight of all the unspoken emotions made her body seem leaden. Her appetite had disappeared, her days seemed long, and her nights even longer. All she could do was replay every moment with the woman who held her heart hostage.

When Dasher entered, her mother was sitting up in her bed looking cheerful. Since her surgery she'd been that way—chatty and, well, motherly. She fussed over Dasher and tried to get her to smile and laugh.

So here she was, miserable. Kate was gone. Dasher registered that her mother was calling her name.

"What? Oh, I'm sorry, Mom. How are you feeling today?" Best to keep the subject light and focused on Mimi, because Dasher wasn't sure how she could hold herself together otherwise.

"I asked where Katie was." From the look on her face her mother was well aware of what Dasher was thinking.

"Haven't talked to her. I don't even know where she is. Go figure." She tried to hide her hurt and anger by keeping her face still and studying her PDA.

After a long silence, Mimi said, "I'm sorry, Dash. Do you think the crazy Pate family finally overwhelmed her?"

Mimi clearly hadn't asked the question to bring the subject back to herself. She seemed genuinely worried. "I don't think so, Mom. She really likes you. Don't doubt that. It was probably me."

Her eyes welled and tears threatened to spill down her face, something that never happened around her mother. Dash had always been the problem solver, not the problem itself. She jumped up and walked to the window, embarrassed by her lack of control.

"Dasher, come here." Her mother's voice was strong and Dasher automatically returned to her side.

Mimi took her hand and held it for a few seconds. The warmth immediately made Dasher relax a bit. It had been years since they'd held hands, but the child she had been had never forgotten her mother's touch, especially the few reassuring ones.

Mimi seemed to search Dasher's face. "You're in love with Kate. What are you planning to do about it?"

Shrugging, Dasher said, "There's not much I can do. She's disappeared."

"Do you know where she is?" Her mother's eyes were steady and warm.

"Probably at the hotel. The one in San Francisco owned by her sister and my friend Stefanie. She goes there a lot."

"Is there a way to know for certain if she's there?"

Dasher had thought about calling Stefanie more times than she could count, but didn't want to drag them into her misery.

"I don't want Stefanie to feel awkward about it. That's not fair."

Her mother became agitated. "Dasher Pate, have you ever heard the expression 'all's fair in love and war'?"

"But—"

"Stop being so freaking honorable and go after her! I mean it, she needs you."

At that moment Dasher's cell phone vibrated. She had forgotten to turn it off in the hospital. Actually, she'd refused to, in case Kate called. She prayed she hadn't just whacked someone because of her negligence.

Mimi looked hopeful and Dasher couldn't get the phone out of her pocket without fumbling a few times.

"It's a text message."

"What does it say?"

Dasher stared at the small screen. "It's from Stef. It says, 'She's here.'"

CHAPTER FIFTEEN

Laurel and Stefanie stared across the table at Kate as she picked at her poached egg on dry toast. Laurel couldn't fathom why she'd ordered such a tasteless meal, especially since she was bordering on too thin. She seemed lost in her own world, barely acknowledging their futile attempts at small talk.

Kate had either stayed in her room or stuck on sunglasses and a Giants baseball cap, as well as an old flannel shirt worn at the cuffs and baggy jeans, and wandered the hills and wharfs of San Francisco. Few recognized her in that disguise, especially with no makeup and her hair carelessly stuffed into the cap. If someone did, she denied that she was a famous star and scurried back to the hotel, ordering room service for the rest of the day. Sika let them know that Kate barely touched the meals.

Laurel eyed Stef, then gently prodded her under the table with her knee to get her attention. When she snapped out of her own reverie and met Laurel's gaze, Laurel could see the worry in Stef's expression, and maybe a little nervousness. Laurel tried to subtly tilt her head toward the exit, hoping she wouldn't have to manually throw Stef out of the dining area.

Stef seemed to finally remember the plan they'd discussed in bed that morning and cleared her throat.

"Well, I'd better get going. I have a punch list a mile long. You two have some fun today." She pushed her chair back and gave Laurel a brief but tender kiss, then squeezed Kate's shoulder as she passed by her.

Gazing at Stef until she disappeared around a corner, Laurel turned back to the table and was surprised to catch Kate watching them. Usually Kate would unblinkingly study her food if Laurel and Stef were affectionate. This time she seemed close to tears and glanced away.

Laurel took her hand. "Kate, what is it? What's bothering you? You suddenly appear and haven't said more than fifty words since you got here."

"You told me you needed help with the final preparations for the hotel, and here I am. End of story." Her voice was flat and lifeless.

Sighing, Laurel muttered, "Keep telling yourself that." She had a million things to do to get ready for the opening and here she was, yet again, listening to another of Kate's dramas. This was getting old.

Kate's eyes flashed. "You're welcome. Listen, just because your life is perfect and you have everything you've ever wanted doesn't mean others are so lucky. So back off."

"Kate, what are you talking about? Everything I've ever wanted? If I recall, *you* are the golden one in the family. You have always been the star, always been the most popular, the best. Now *I'm* the one with everything? Where's this coming from?"

Looking ready to pounce, Kate snapped, "You tell me. Tell me you aren't happy. Tell me you aren't in love. Tell me you can't be exactly who you are. Tell me!"

Laurel sat back, stunned at the pain she detected in Kate's

accusations. Suddenly Kate closed her eyes and put her face in her hands, elbows on the table. Whatever energy she was using to fight had disappeared.

"Katie, I'm sorry. I thought you were the happiest woman on earth. You've always had everything you've ever desired. You're beautiful, rich, famous, and everybody envies you. Now tell me which one of those Hollywood bad boys you're upset with and we'll figure out how to dump him." Laurel doubted her words, but this was Kate's usual pattern.

Holding up a hand, Kate gave her a sad smile. "You don't envy me, though, do you, Laur." It wasn't a question.

Taken aback, Laurel could only be honest. "I used to. I mean, you always had a lot of attention. But I suppose the answer is no, I don't envy you. I have no idea how you live up to all those expectations. I should thank you, because having all that attention focused on you allowed me to get by. Although I've always suspected that Mom and Dad were disappointed with the lesbian thing."

"Oh, God." Everything Laurel said seemed to upset Kate more.

Laurel slipped into her protective big-sister role. Something was definitely different about Kate. Usually her unannounced entrances were brief and filled with drama. This time Kate had arrived quietly and stayed to herself most of the time. Laurel touched Kate's arm. "What's wrong?"

Kate automatically glanced around the room. The dining room had closed for breakfast an hour earlier and Kate had appeared only then. Since the hotel was in its shakedown phase, not many knew it was open. Apparently satisfied that no one was around, Kate met Laurel's concerned gaze with the red-rimmed eyes of a woman who had been crying for a long time. Laurel waited, sensing something extraordinary was about to happen.

"I think I'm in love."

There it was. Katie was in love. But why the stealth? Why the tears? She'd uttered those precious words like her announcement was a tragedy. Laurel suspected the answer but decided to proceed carefully.

"Well, that's wonderful, right?" Kate's expression filled with raw anguish, and as much as she wanted to comfort her baby sister, she knew she had to wait for her to continue.

After what seemed like a long time Kate sniffed loudly and met her gaze. "Tell me about Rochelle."

Laurel was speechless. This conversation had taken a decided turn. Was Kate actually asking her about her abusive ex-partner? Was someone hitting Kate? Why was this subject coming up now?

After taking a breath, Laurel kept talking. "Remember the last time you visited Rochelle and me in Berkeley? When you wanted to get rid of your latest dating disaster and were afraid he'd get to the tabloids first?"

Jerkily nodding, Kate shivered.

"Rochelle always had a crush on you, always made a fool of herself when you were around. I knew she made you uncomfortable." Laughing mirthlessly, Laurel added, "Her behavior was humiliating."

Kate took her hand and seemed to steel herself for the question she asked next. "Did that woman hurt you?"

"Not then, at least not that much. But she escalated." Laurel had automatically tried to shield Kate and not paint Rochelle in such stark colors. Perhaps she was still embarrassed that she'd chosen such a violent partner. But no longer. The next step was Kate's. If she reacted like she always had, she'd simply accept that answer and move on.

Kate took a breath and Laurel recognized the determination in her expression. "Tell me."

Quietly, with little inflection, Laurel released Kate's hand and hugged herself as she went down that painful path. "She was jealous and possessive. She demeaned me when she could. I knew she was screwing around on me with students, but she told me I was worthless without her. At first, she contented herself with verbal abuse, but the more she drank and the more I stepped out from her shadow, the more physical she became."

"That bitch." Kate was clenching her hands into fists.

Laurel thought about reassuring her, but Kate had asked, and Laurel needed to finish this. "The day you were there she only shoved me and told me to never embarrass her again by implying she wasn't welcome in our conversation. When she found out I had discovered papers that revealed the hotel's past and kept them from her, she beat me. She didn't even know about Stef." Laurel smiled slightly, as if seeing her partner's image in front of her.

"This hotel, as ramshackle as it was then, was my refuge." Laurel managed to gather herself. "The women here were *my* friends, and Stef was my salvation. I fell in love with her. Eventually I found the courage to tell Rochelle I was leaving. I thought she would kill me, Kate. I really did. I found my way back to the hotel and Stefanie, and that's when my life really began."

By that time both of them were crying and hugging. Kate said, "Laur, I'm so sorry. I should have realized that if she creeped me out, she was even worse for you. I've been so absorbed in me for so long. I apologize."

Laurel wiped her nose with a napkin. "I guess, in the long run, it all worked out. I learned that I have to stand up for myself. And if anyone finds love, real love, she should grab it and hold on for dear life. She should never let anyone tell her who to be."

Laurel watched the anguish on Kate's face ratchet up another level. "Kate, why did you want to know all that? Is someone hurting you?"

Shaking her head, Kate said, "Laurel, I think I'm a lesbian."

They sat in silence for a moment. Finally, Laurel ventured, "You're in love with Dasher Pate."

Kate's head whipped around to meet her gaze. "How did you know?"

"Well, did you open the package I sent with the proof sheets from the photo shoot? Some of them were, um, lens-fogging."

Nodding slowly, Kate reacted as if that question threatened to sever the final tendril that was keeping her from coming apart. She absently rubbed the flannel material of the shirt she'd worn every day since her arrival. Her eyes began to well.

Laurel abruptly stood and took her hand. "Come on, not here. Let's go to your room."

They hurried through the kitchen past a silent Sika Phelps, who stood chopping vegetables and seemed not to notice them. Laurel knew Sika never missed a thing and suspected she was merely giving Kate her own space.

Once in the private elevator, Kate said, "I'll bet Sika heard every word."

"Probably." Laurel was preparing to assure her that Sika would never divulge anything, but Kate just nodded as if she already knew. Kate, who trusted so few, seemed to trust the women of the hotel, including Laurel.

Laurel was surprised at how relieved she was to finally share that awful part of her life with Kate. And she was even more surprised, and gratified, that Kate had wanted to know.

Once inside Kate's suite, they sat down on the couch and Kate squeezed her hands together as if waiting to hear a prison sentence. Laurel waited because Kate had to be the one to say her own truth.

"Ironically, I don't even know if she loves me. I mean, Mom and Dad will be heartbroken, Joe will shoot me, my fans will disown me, my career is over, but all I'm worried about is if she loves me back. What a joke."

Okay, that was a beginning.

"Kate, have you told her about your feelings for her?"

"God, no. What if she laughed at me? What if she told all her friends what a fool I am? What if she—"

"Told you she loves you, too?"

Kate recoiled as though scalded. She stared at Laurel and then flopped back on the couch. "Oh my God. What if she does love me?"

Noticing Kate's cell phone vibrating across the coffee table and Kate regarding it guiltily, Laurel asked, "Does she know where you are?"

Kate only shook her head, eyes riveted to the phone.

"She must be worried."

That seemed to be all it took, because Kate leapt at the cell and answered it.

"Hello? Oh, Joe. Yes, I'm out of town. I'm in San Francisco helping my sister. Don't worry, Joe. I've handled all the interviews. No, I won't be back for a while. I've got to go." Laurel could hear him squawking at the other end as Kate ended the call.

"When do you plan to fire that man?"

Sighing, Kate said, "When I signed with him he told me I didn't need to sign a contract sanctioned by the Screen Actors Guild because his was much better and, like a fool, I believed him. He's got me until he releases me, period. Believe me, I've had attorneys look at the contract."

"Damn. And you signed with him because—"

"Because Dasher Pate made me feel things I'd never experienced before and it scared the hell out of me. Because I'm an idiot. A fucking idiot. There, how's that for a revelation?"

"Has Dasher called you?"

"Yes."

"Have you talked?"

"No. I haven't picked up."

Laurel sighed in frustration. "Kate. Figure out your relationship first, then worry about the rest. And I would strongly suggest you work this out *with* Dasher, not by imagining what she is or isn't thinking."

Seeing the trepidation in Kate's eyes, she added, "Buck up, little sis. You're very brave. You can do this. I say so, and I'm your big sister."

Snorting, Kate gravely replied, "Yeah. You and Eleanor Roosevelt."

Judging by the look on Kate's face, she thought Laurel should understand her strange statement. Laurel stuffed her question and kissed her on the top of her head, like she had when they were kids and she needed to calm her. "Are you going to call Dasher?"

Kate picked up the phone and pressed a number she obviously knew by heart, then finally left a message for Dasher to call her and looked hopelessly at Laurel.

Offering her hand, Laurel hefted Kate to her feet. "Come on, let's go see if Stef needs us for anything, then maybe we can ditch work for a few hours."

Kate looked close to tears. "Thanks, sis. I think I need the distraction. I may have permanently screwed this up."

"Maybe not. At least you got the ball rolling."

They rode the elevator down in silence. Laurel was already planning a few errands they could run together when the doors opened on the ground floor.

There, standing beside Stefanie, was Dasher Pate. Stef's eyes went round, then she pulled Laurel out and gently shoved Dasher inside the lift. "Have fun."

The door closed with the two of them staring at one another.

Laurel turned to Stef. "How?"

"I sent her a text message."

"Why?"

"Because I knew if Kate was this miserable, Dasher had to be."

"But Kate just told me she was in love with Dasher. How did you—?"

Sighing theatrically, Stefanie said, "She's your sister, Laur. For all of her worldly ego stuff, she's a lot like you. Five years ago Dasher told me about a woman who broke her heart. Then Kate marches in with some cockamamie story about meeting Dasher five years before. Oh, and I have eyes."

The silence that followed made Stefanie fidget, but Laurel wanted a minute to appreciate what her thoughtful partner had just done. Finally, Laurel gave her a ghost of a grin. "Well, at least this way they'll finally know, without the prying eyes of the paparazzi."

"Honey, you do realize that if this thing goes south, we've probably lost our star for opening night. And I'll have lost a good friend in Dasher and my future sister-in-law, whom I was beginning to like."

Stef seemed lost in doubt when Laurel abruptly pinned her to the wall beside the elevator and covered her face with kisses. She returned the favor but finally held her back and asked, "So I'm forgiven?"

"Did you just propose?" Laurel waited, wanting to know for sure if she had heard the words correctly.

"Well I…I…think I did. Wow, that was easy." Stef seemed

astounded at what she'd just said. "But it feels right, Laurel. Will you? Marry me?"

Laurel got very close to Stef's ear and whispered, "Yes."

Stef turned Laurel around so she could ring for the elevator. As they rode up to their suite, she said, "Sometimes it's the reply that makes a question perfect."

Kate slid the key through the lock, receiving a green light as the lock disengaged. With Dasher standing just behind her she had the sensation that time had slowed and noises had intensified. The lock had the report of a cannon.

"Come in." Her voice was definitely shaky, and she was having a difficult time not trembling. Taking a few steps, she turned to see Dasher still in the doorway looking very unsure of herself. "Dasher, I can't do this alone. Either come in or leave."

Kate blinked, and when she opened her eyes, the door was closed and Dasher was within kissing distance. Kate had resolved to have that talk before she could even contemplate touching. She well knew what happened when she had any type of physical contact with Dasher. Her mind was hopping around like a disturbed monkey at this point, but if she felt Dasher's skin, all bets were off. She had to be rational about this.

Dasher obviously failed to read her mind because she tentatively raised her hand and ran her thumb the length of Kate's eyebrow, then cupped her face in her strong hands. The hands that Kate had fantasized about since their campout.

She melted into the touch, memorizing the incredible feel of their warmth. She was so absorbed in that moment that when Dasher's lips grazed hers she gasped and her eyes flew open to drown in the gray-blue depths that invited her. "Oh!"

"I want more than a kiss." Dasher's voice was husky, her fingers telegraphing the slightest tremble.

Kate searched her face for deception, her eyes for a look she knew well. Too often her suitors had wanted the exterior, not caring at all about the person she was inside. She saw none of that. What she did see made her heart hammer in her chest, probably because all her blood was draining to another pulse point.

"What do you want, Dasher? Who are you looking for?" She held her breath, waiting for something she'd never experienced before.

"I want you, Kate. I'm looking for you. Only you."

Their lips met in astounding softness, and their tongues touched in a delicate dance that stole her breath. She slid her arms around Dasher's neck and pulled her into a deep embrace, broken only by her need to take a breath.

"Dasher, I've never done this with a woman before. I've thought of it, but never—"

"We don't have to *do* anything."

Kate was at once relieved and irritated. And aroused—undeniably, horribly, wonderfully aroused. "The hell we don't. Dasher Pate, if you don't touch me right now I'll never speak to you again. I mean it."

She was about to launch into a diatribe when Dasher swept her into her arms, marched her into the bedroom, and tossed her on the bed. She removed her jacket, the one Kate remembered from the photo shoot. Kate watched as she shed her shoes, then turned and gently took Kate's off as well.

Dasher climbed in the bed and lay beside her. She ran her fingers along the sleeve of the shirt Kate was wearing.

"I wondered what had happened to this shirt. I hoped you had it."

Kate knew she was probably blushing, but she told the truth. "I've only been out of this shirt to shower since I've been up here. I needed it."

Dasher smiled tenderly. "Then it's yours. Anything I have is yours."

She pulled Kate on top of her. They regarded each other silently, then Dasher reversed their positions and her weight on Kate was exhilarating. It was as though all these years Kate had been afloat, aimlessly drifting through space, and now she was tethered and grounded.

The kisses started slowly, languorously. First her lips, her eyes, her ears. Oh, her ears. By the time Dasher reached her neck, Kate was squirming.

"Dasher, please." At that moment Dasher ground her pelvis into Kate's, and that did it. Kate was accustomed to acting passionate for a film, but suddenly her clothes were too tight and she had to feel Dasher next to her, skin to skin.

She pulled Dasher's shirt from her jeans, and the two of them scrambled out of their clothes within seconds. Dasher stopped the moment they were both naked and stared reverently at Kate. Her eyes shone as she said, "My God, Kate. You are so lovely."

Immediately shy, Kate said, "Oh, Dash, if you've seen any of my films you've probably seen most of it before." She'd done a few topless shots at Joe's urging and they were circulated endlessly on the Internet. She hated that.

"No. That was the actress. I want only you."

Those words melted Kate's bones and flooded her with emotion. Dasher eased Kate back on the bed and settled between her legs, tentatively at first. She must have felt Kate's wetness because her breath caught and her pupils darkened. They kissed again, this time not holding back. She moved to torture each nipple with her tongue and teeth and worshipped them by pulling them into her mouth.

Kate had never enjoyed men touching her breasts, perhaps because that seemed to be all they thought about, that and bragging to their buddies that they had "nailed" Kate Hoffman. But when Dasher's lips touched her nipples, she arched toward her for more.

Kate felt Dasher's passion when she dripped on her clitoris, and that only took her higher. She reached between them and almost came when she felt how swollen and wet Dasher was. Had she done this? Was the passion just for Kate?

"Kate, I can't hold off if you do that. It's been so long." Dasher was panting and held herself up and back.

"I don't want you to hold back. Ever." She was almost desperate to have this moment, as though it might be their only one. She stroked the swollen flesh, then plunged inside this beautiful woman she knew she loved. She wanted their first time together to begin with her pleasuring Dasher.

Dasher stilled, then curled forward and shook. "Katie!" Then she pumped repeatedly onto Kate's hand and Kate watched, drunk with power of a very different kind than she had ever known. The intoxication came from making Dasher feel these things, from knowing that her love had caused Dasher to crash into oblivion.

Dasher collapsed onto Kate and Kate held her, tears of joy in her eyes. Finally, Kate knew what falling in love was all about, was certain that she was in love with Dasher.

After a few moments, Dasher began to trace a trail down Kate's stomach with her tongue and Kate thought about telling her to stop. But Dasher parted her and stroked the length of her before taking her swollen clitoris in her mouth to tug and suck on it. Her fingers slipped inside and then she used the tip of her tongue to assault the head of Kate's clit. Just before Kate came she managed to look down at Dasher, and what she saw in her eyes filled her with so much emotion she stopped worrying that Dasher might not return her love. Then Kate lost her mind.

They continued making love until the early morning hours when, exhausted, they fell asleep. After a short time Kate slipped out of bed and found her phone she'd vaguely registered vibrating on the table the night before. The text message was from Joe Alder.

> *I'll ruin you both if you screw that cunt. You know I can do it. Get your ass back here.*

Tears streamed down her face as she sat alone in a corner of the sofa, trying to think of a way to save Dasher from Alder's viciousness. Leaving seemed to be her only option, but that seemed impossible now.

❖

Dasher reached for Kate and found the bed empty but the spot still warm. Panicked, she jackknifed up to search for Kate. She wasn't in the bedroom and there was no light on in the bathroom.

Flying to the doorway she saw Kate, naked and huddled in a corner of the couch, quietly sobbing. She couldn't have been there long. What had happened to upset her so much? Had she pushed Kate too far? Perhaps Kate regretted their night together. Dasher couldn't breathe; she would hurt herself before she would hurt Kate.

"Kate?" Dasher went to her and took her in her arms, holding tight, feeling her warm tears on her breast while her own heart broke. Kate clung to her.

She knew she had to withdraw and let Kate make her

decisions, but she couldn't help kissing her face, tracing the tears, crooning gentle nonsense to her to try to comfort her. She'd never love another woman, but she had to let Kate go, and her own tears soon mingled with Kate's.

Burrowing into Dasher's embrace, Kate sought her touch, her gentle kisses, which made her whole. She had to go back to LA, to handle her life, and maybe then she could offer Dasher something more than the mess she had created. If only she'd had the courage to love this woman five years ago.

Feeling Dasher's tears she opened her eyes and saw terrible sadness on Dasher's face. "Dash, tell me."

"I didn't mean to push you. I didn't want to force you into making love with me. I'm sorry."

Staring, Kate said, "What are you talking about?" Warning bells sounded in her head, urging her to be quiet, not say how she felt. This was the perfect out. But she couldn't, wouldn't let Dasher think that she was responsible. She'd had enough of that in her life. "All my life people have used me to get something for themselves. You have never done that. Dasher, I love you. Last night was the best night of my life. Are you listening?"

Dasher was mentally preparing to pack and leave when the words began to make inroads in her misery. Her heart stuttered, stopped, then roared almost out of her chest. "I love you, too!" She sounded like a pubescent teenager but didn't care.

They fell together, full of laughter mixed with the tears. Dash had never felt such joy. Abruptly she held Kate away from her and asked, "You were crying and I thought I was the cause. If not, why?"

The fear that crossed Kate's beautiful eyes made Dasher want to tear something to pieces. Dasher ground out, "Joe Alder. What did he do? I'm going to kill him."

A smile tugged at Kate's lovely mouth, then vanished. She reached for her phone and brought up the text message. Dasher read it, her face frozen by the time she realized what this could mean.

"You aren't leaving. You aren't giving in to this man."

Kate put a hand on her chest and a finger on her lips. "He's not welcome in our bedroom. Not now, not ever. He can't spoil the night we had." She caressed Dasher's breast, allowing her thumb to tease the nipple to attention. "Are you cold, darling?"

"Not anymore."

Kate watched Dasher's eyes turn from gray to indigo and touched her lips, swollen from the night before. She let her hands continue to explore the beautiful body that was still new to her. She wanted to know every inch of it: all of the tickle spots, all of the erogenous zones, every imperfection, every story. Then she planned to write a few of her own.

She reached to the magical vee between Dasher's legs and thrilled at the passion gathered there. Slipping inside Dash, she pulled up, reveling in the gasp she received. Dasher called her name and sagged against her, making her whole body tingle in anticipation of Dasher's climax.

"No." Dasher stilled her hand. "You. You are mine." She seemed barely able to choke the words out but determined to say them.

Time stopped.

Kate thought she might faint when Dasher sat back and delicately flicked her swollen clitoris with her thumb, then placed pressure right where Kate needed it. Suddenly, Dasher was everywhere, in every cell, taking away any self-control she thought she had. She came, wondering if perhaps she screamed, because the waves of sensation didn't stop and nothing existed in her universe but Dasher and the love she had just given and claimed.

When she could open her eyes again, Dasher lay next to her, gazing with such love that she ached from its fullness. "Did you come, too?"

A slight nod and a smile told her *yes, but*. She cupped Dasher and found her drenched. "But not enough."

The sun was peeking out from the fog by the time they slept again. They explored the limits of their passion and found none.

Chapter Sixteen

He can't do a thing to me. The only way he can hurt me is by hurting you, and I won't let that happen," Dasher said. They had managed to get out of the bed and actually showered—together, then separately.

"I've tried to break the contract, Dasher. He has to consent and he won't. What he *will* do is make sure I get shit jobs until I'm old enough to play Mrs. Robinson seducing some teenager. He's not above doing that. He'll also plant rumors and innuendo about you in all the rags, online, you name it. He'll try to undermine your list of talent. I've seen him do that with lesser-known names, and he's succeeded. He hates you."

"Yeah, I know. The more successful my clients, the more he clings to you. When I went to visit you in the hospital, he told me he'd have me arrested if I ever approached you again."

"Hospital? What hospital?" Kate thought back to her knee injury. "Did you come see me when I was injured? I must have been out of it or I'd remember."

When Dasher nodded absently, her creased brow told Kate that she was barely listening. Kate had dreamt Dasher was there, holding her hand. Then she vanished and Kate was left with a feeling of desolation when she woke up with only Joe there to yap at her.

Her phone sounded. They exchanged a look and she jumped when it warbled again. Tentatively she reached for it and checked the screen. "It's a text from Laurel."

After opening the message she read it and started laughing and, judging from the warmth on her neck, blushing. She handed Dasher the phone.

> *Hey, you two. Want to meet for breakfast? Brunch? Lunch? DINNER? Should we send in oxygen? We could dine in our suite so not everyone will tease you. Yet.*
>
> *Sincerely, your sister Laurel and her FIANCEE Stefanie*

Dasher was turning a nice shade of pink when she yelped, "Katie! Stefanie must have proposed to Laurel. Well, I'll be damned. I never thought anyone would get Stef to the altar."

Grabbing the phone, Kate read it twice more. "Laurel is something else. She's my hero. She and Eleanor Roosevelt got me to invite you to my room last night."

Only vaguely aware of Dasher's head cocked to one side, she immediately texted back, then handed the phone to Dash to approve. It was natural to want her input. What a marvel. Oh, and she really loved it when Dasher called her Katie.

> *Ahem. Congratulations! Of course we'd love to meet you for...dinner. Say 6:30? Love, K and D*

Dasher looked it over and nodded. Raising an eyebrow,

she said, "You know, that's five hours from now. We might starve to death."

Kate grinned. "That's what mini-bars are for. Let's see what they've got because I have plans for you."

"Let's make that eight o'clock," Dasher mumbled as she reached for the phone.

Kate threw the phone on the table. "Like it or not, we have to emerge sometime."

Just then someone knocked on the door. Kate checked through the peephole and saw Ember Jones, sensational in a form-fitting black-and-white uniform, standing behind a food cart. She idly wondered if Ember prepared the food as well, then washed the dishes afterward.

Making sure they both were wearing something, she swung the door open. Ember, refusing to make eye contact and blushing a nice shade of magenta, pushed the cart into the room.

She stood back and grinned, then announced to the ceiling, "Compliments of the Hotel Liaison, our emergency cart," and vanished.

The cart contained five different appetizers, along with tea, coffee, water, and sodas. The note said, "Hydrate. Eat. You'll need your strength. See you soon, Laurel."

"My sister is getting way too much fun out of this."

Sliding her arms around Kate's waist, Dasher whispered, "Not nearly as much as we are."

"Good point."

At 6:30 they knocked on the door to Stefanie and Laurel's suite, and Laurel threw the door open just as Stef popped the

cork on a bottle of champagne. Once each of them held a flute of bubbly, Stefanie said, "To love. Forever, love."

They toasted and drank, and Kate noticed that they all seemed to glow with optimism. "Say, when did you get engaged?"

Laurel said, "About the same time you got laid."

"Laurel!" Kate was amazed. Her shy bookworm sister? Both Dasher and Stef were coughing, and Stefanie seemed to have gotten some bubbles up her nose.

Folding her arms, Kate commented, "Looks like we all accomplished that feat."

Laurel started giggling and finally held up her hand. "Okay, okay, truce."

Stefanie said, "We're really happy for you two. Now tell us, how do you plan to handle Joe Alder?"

Sobering and glancing to each other, Dasher said, "Other than putting a hit out on him, any suggestions?"

For the next half hour they shared everything that had been happening, including showing them Joe's text message.

"That disgusting man," Laurel said. "Surely we can take care of him."

A bell signaling a new text-message arrival rang for both Dasher and Kate. Kate's stomach clenched as she saw it was from Joe, with attachments. Her face must have said it all because Laurel and Stef gathered around.

The message read, *You have 24 hours or I release these on the Internet.*

Three photos were attached: one of Dasher and Kate walking on the beach in Malibu and two of two women together, topless, from a distance, vaguely resembling Dasher and Kate.

"That bastard! Those paparazzi who've been following me must have taken the first one. They hung around the hospital where Dash's mother is being treated. Now we know who they work for. The last two are nothing more than trumped-up garbage."

From across the room Dasher quietly said, "But this isn't."

They all looked as she held up her phone to show a video playing on it. As they crowded close to the small screen, they watched a very young Greta Sarnoff give a man a blow job. She seemed spaced out, drugged, perhaps. She couldn't have been more than twelve or thirteen, and she looked half-starved.

Kate said, "Poor Greta. Joe sent this to you?" She was afraid she would vomit.

"Yes. With the promise to release it if I see you again."

Laurel stared in horror. Stef was pacing back and forth, her hands clenched behind her back.

Kate looked around the room and knew what she had to do. Alder planned to try to destroy not only her, but Dasher and now even Greta. Enough was enough.

She pulled out her phone and punched a number. When someone answered she identified herself and said, "Please send a limo to the Hotel Liaison immediately. Destination? San Francisco International."

"Kate? What are you doing?" Laurel said. "We're going to do all we can to help."

Gazing into Dasher's eyes, perhaps for the last time, Kate shook her head. "No, this is my mess, and I've jeopardized all of you because of it. Even Greta, who, God knows, doesn't deserve any more tragedy in her life. I won't do it. All I have to do is go back. Dasher, I…apologize."

With that she was gone.

Laurel started for the door but Dasher's voice stopped her "Let her go. If she's not willing to try, there's nothing I can do."

After another minute of stunned silence Dasher stood and said, "If you'll excuse me." She closed the door behind her.

"Well, that went well." Stefanie took Laurel's hand. "Are you willing to forget about this?"

Laurel pulled her into a searing kiss. "Absolutely not. Let's divide the list and start calling. Time for a meeting of Elysium."

Chapter Seventeen

Kate slammed the front door of her home, opened it, and slammed it two more times. She'd been back in LA for a week and hadn't heard from Dasher, Laurel, or Stefanie. Joe was smug and demanding, and she realized that he would only get worse. He'd always have the threat to hold over her head.

She couldn't fall asleep because the erotic memories of her time with Dash kept her awake, and when she did sleep she had nightmares of being naked and defenseless with Joe Alder getting ready to do awful things to her. During the day her mind circled endlessly as she tried to figure out how to get away from Alder and back into Dasher's arms.

Knowing she looked a wreck and not caring, she'd run twice as long as she normally did along the beach. She'd avoided Dasher's stretch of shoreline, but the need for Dasher was becoming more unbearable by the minute.

"Why is it that when I finally fall in love I can't be with the person I'm meant for? Why? My parents? They'll get over it. My career? I quit. My fans? Some will stay, others won't, who cares?"

Here she was, ready to give up fame and fortune for love, and she couldn't even do that right. Joe must have realized she was willing to let it all go and figured out a way to hold on to her. All he had to do was threaten Dasher and Greta. Who knew Kate would actually have ethics? Wasn't most of Hollywood amoral? What was wrong with *her*? She knew damned good and well that she couldn't live with herself if she hurt Dash or Greta. Damn it all to hell.

She didn't even register the doorbell until it rang at least ten times and someone began to pound on the door. The noise finally pulled her from her concentration, and she cursed whichever reporter or delivery person might be standing out there. Now she wouldn't be able to stop herself from thinking about Dash again.

She stomped to the door and flung it open. There, on the front stoop, stood Mimi Pate. Behind her was Dasher's father, Jerry.

"Mimi?" It had only been a few weeks since the surgery, and it must have taken a toll on her to come here to see Kate. From the redness of Jerry's face, it was he who had pounded on the door. Kate felt guilty because she'd avoided calling even Mimi.

Mimi wobbled slightly and Kate immediately took her elbow, looking past Jerry Pate to their car, hoping Dasher was with them. It was empty and her heart sank. She'd blown it for good this time. Even if she could find a solution to the Joe problem, Dasher would never forgive her for running out on her again.

"Please, come in."

She raised an eyebrow at Jerry, and he shook his head and shoved his hands into the pockets of his jeans. "I'm gonna go for a walk."

Kate couldn't tell if he was mad at her or what he was feeling, since he had that tall, silent thing going on. She was really too distraught to care, but assumed he would cheerfully strangle her for hurting his daughter. Odd, that thought was strangely comforting. She didn't know if the notion of him strangling her or his protectiveness of Dasher appealed to her more.

Mimi moved slowly but determinedly into the family room of the house and sat down on a chair with a big sigh. She motioned for Kate to sit opposite her. "I hope we aren't breaking any of Joe Alder's rules by showing up here. After all, we *are* related to Dasher." She seemed amused at the idea.

Embarrassed at her all-too-apparent cowardice, Kate said, "Mimi, you're always welcome. I'm surprised, that's all. I thought you were agoraphobic."

"Yes, well, it's true I haven't been out in a while, mostly because I was too drunk or stoned to move. But I have to try, now, don't I? I promised Dasher before the surgery."

An awkward silence fell between them. Finally, Kate had to ask, had to know. "Mimi, how is Dasher? Is she okay?"

Mimi's eyes hardened for a moment, then softened. "Kate, she'd be mad at me for saying this, but she's devastated. She called the other day to check in and fell apart on the phone when I asked about you."

"Oh, Mimi, I miss her so much. But I can't risk her career and Greta Sarnoff's, too. I presume Dasher told you what Joe Alder threatened. I don't care if I ever perform again. I just wish I could find a way to be with Dasher."

"You and I are in a similar position, then." Mimi let that one lie there between them.

"What do you mean?" She couldn't see *any* resemblance. What drugs did they have Mimi on?

"Well, I've been a shut-in for years, making everybody miserable, most of all myself. But I took the risk to try and make a new life, *outside* of the cave I'd hidden myself in. I might not have done it if it wasn't for you and Dasher, and

I still might have chickened out if I hadn't heard the misery in Dasher's voice. Even Jerry is worried enough to leave his work and try to help. We're both in this place because of you two."

Confused, Kate said, "Thank you?"

"You're welcome. It's a start." Mimi smiled as if she hoped everything would turn out well for everyone.

"I still don't see—"

"Kate, how much of the past month is new territory for you? Do you have new friends?"

Kate nodded.

"Are you in love?"

Her breath caught in her throat as she nodded again.

"Are you doing things that are completely out of your safety zone?"

"Yes, yes, yes! I don't even recognize me. And no matter how hard I try, I can't seem to do the right thing. I know I have to leave Dasher or I'll be risking everything for both of us, not even counting poor Greta. But all I really want to do is be with her. I want her forever, Mimi. I don't care about anything else. What am I going to do?"

Mimi held out her arms and Kate collapsed into them, convulsed with sobs. "No matter what I do, I think I may have lost her."

After Kate calmed to the point of just a few hiccups, Mimi said, "You have to try, Kate. Ask her. Ask Greta. Let them answer for themselves. If the answer is no, then at least you know."

"But…Joe swore he'd—"

"This is your life, not Joe's. You cannot be his victim. He'll never stop demanding things from you. There will always be a Joe around, if you allow it. Is that what you want?"

Kate violently shook her head but had no words. The time

for those had passed. Mimi had voiced what had been in her mind for the past week. If Dasher would take her back, they'd find a way together.

She kissed Mimi on the cheek and stood, helping her to her feet. Looking directly in her eyes, she said, "Thank you. Wish me luck."

"I do, sweetheart. I want you in this family. You're the only person who can heal Dasher's heart. I hope she knows that, too."

She walked out front with Mimi and Jerry and waved good-bye to them. Jerry looked grim but was listening intently to Mimi and fiddling with his phone when they pulled away from the house.

Kate went to the bathroom and splashed some water on her face. "You still look like shit." She changed from her sweats to jeans and a top, rubbed the fabric of the precious flannel shirt for luck, grabbed a windbreaker, and was out the door.

Meeting a welcoming committee was the last thing she had expected today.

Dasher drove listlessly down the Pacific Coast Highway to her home. She wasn't looking forward to another dreary evening. She'd tried getting drunk, but all she got for it was a hangover. She busied herself with work, but somehow it didn't do the trick, either. She was afraid it would be a long time before anything mattered.

Pulling into the drive, she set the brake, locked the car, and let herself into her house, tossing her keys and the mail from the door slot onto the table beside the door. All she had scheduled today was a meeting with Greta, who'd called earlier and said she would come to Dasher's house. Dasher had told her about the video, and Greta hadn't said a word. She left the front door open and the screen door unlocked so Greta could let herself inside.

Picking up the mail, she shuffled into the main room of her small house, dividing the mail into junk and business. But a sudden movement outside caught her attention and she looked out the slider in back. Her breath caught in her chest. A woman was walking from the oceanfront toward her house. She couldn't distinguish her features yet, but she recognized the walk. She had spent so many restless nights dreaming about that walk.

She told herself she was just wishing it to be the way she had fantasized for so long. This was the tenth time she'd imagined some stranger to be Kate. Maybe one day she'd stop doing that.

Still, she couldn't resist hurrying out to her deck to get a better look. The woman stopped, then slowly removed her baseball cap, allowing her blond hair to billow in the breeze. Next came her sunglasses and there stood Kate.

After keeping her arms crossed for a second or two, Dasher lowered them. God help her, she was so desperate to hold Kate, touch her. Kate took a few more tentative steps toward her, then broke into a run, slowed only by the sand slipping through her toes.

Dasher was off the deck in an instant. Kate took a final leap and landed squarely in Dasher's arms, sending them toppling over into a heap.

Breathless, she managed, "Dasher, I love you. Never leave me again."

They rolled around and, between kisses, Dasher was able to say "never" about a hundred times. Finally, covered in sand, Dasher looked at Kate and said, "I thought *you* left *me*."

"Details." Kate whooped and pulled Dash up to a standing

position. Off to their left they heard the telltale sound of a camera shutter and turned to see Chaz Hockaday, shooting away. Michael stood behind him holding some equipment bags.

"Give me the camera." Dasher had had enough.

Looking offended, Chaz said, "Now, now, you know I can't do that. These shots will—" He took off like a flash when Dasher lunged, but only got about twenty feet before he ran into a brick wall by the name of Jock Reynolds.

"Chaz Hockaday, isn't it? Fancy meeting you here." With that she snatched the Nikon from his hands.

"Hey! That's private property."

"No, you are *on* private property. That means if Ms. Pate wants to press trespassing and harassment charges, she can. Do you have any idea how much Malibu residents value their privacy?"

A small shriek behind them revealed that Denny Phelps had surprised Michael and was confiscating all of his equipment. Chaz started toward them. "Leave him alone!"

Kate looked between the two men. *Of course.* "Are you two a couple?"

Michael looked hopefully at Chaz, who said, "Yes, we are. So what?"

Seeing the joy on Michael's face, Kate filled in quite a few blanks. She glared squarely at Chaz and said, "Well, you're a disgrace to your…your…sexual orientation, that's what."

All eyes were on her. She needed time to think and marched through their group to Dasher's house. Stopping at the door, she dusted herself free of some of the sand that now filled all her orifices and entered, waving imperiously for them to follow. *Ah, bravado, works every time.* She was nervous because so much was at stake, but she refused to let anyone see her fear. Hollywood had taught her a few lessons very well.

Everyone mutely followed and soon they were all sitting in the main room, the two men fidgeting. Jock looked formidable, having chosen to prop herself against the wall next to the sliding doors with her hands stuffed in her pockets and wearing an intense expression on her handsome features. Denny discreetly put herself into position to head off the intruding men should they try to run out the front door.

Kate asked Dasher to order some pizza and beer for all of them, thinking that might relax everybody. She was thoroughly prepared to stuff the pizza down their gullets whole if her ploy failed. Dash gave her a quizzical look, scratched her head, releasing some sand of her own, and picked up the phone.

Kate sat down and got to the point. "How long have you known Joe Alder?"

Chaz folded his arms across his chest. "I don't know who you're talking about."

Sharpening her glare she said, "Dasher, would you call the police to report a trespass and stalking?"

The phone still in her hand, Dasher said, "Alrighty," and started punching in numbers.

Michael yelped, "Wait! Chaz, Joe Alder isn't worth jail time. We've only done this one job for him. We had to follow you and get any sensational material we could."

"Mikey! We have client confidentiality!"

"He's an awful man and you know it." To the group he said, "We've checked him out with the other reporters. He's done stuff like this before, but I swear we didn't help him."

Stepping closer, Jock loomed over the two men. "He's threatening to destroy Kate and Dasher's careers, and he's planning to use your photos to do it. All because they love each other. And you're going to let him?"

Chaz looked down at his hands. "This was our last stakeout, I swear. We'd even talked about just lying and saying we didn't find anything. He's not that interested in you anymore, Miss Hoffman. Now it's all about Miss Pate. He talks like he can call all the shots from now on."

Shock must have registered on Kate's face because Dasher was instantly by her side with a hand on her shoulder asking if she was okay. She said, "He was always meaning to come after you, no matter what I did. Why does he hate you so much?"

From the front door, a familiar voice said, "I can answer that, Kate. Dasher is everything Joe isn't. She is respected, has A-list stars, and you're in love with her. She's on her way up, not clinging to the one actress who still gives him credibility. Worse, she's homosexual. In his mind, that's the only thing lower than he is. Besides, more than Dasher, Kate, he's coming for me." Greta Sarnoff entered, closed the door, and stood beside it.

After her dramatic entrance, she sat down and made deliberate eye contact with each person in the room. She lingered on the men, Chaz in particular. With narrowed eyes and a heavier accent than Kate had ever heard her use she said, "If any of this ends up in a rag, I'll come for you. I'm Russian, don't doubt me."

Chaz and Michael looked like two bobbleheads in their haste to agree.

"What rumors had you heard of this man Joe Alder?"

It wasn't really a question, more a command. Chaz didn't hesitate. "He used to be in the porn business. We also heard he was weird with young girls."

Jock, who had finally sat down, started from her seat. "You knew the sonofabitch was a pedophile and you still worked for him?" The well-defined muscles in her forearms stood out as she gripped the chair arms. Kate thought she might hurl it at the men.

Chaz held up his hands. "Look, the job didn't involve kids.

The rumors were just that—rumors. The money was so good we…I…took it. Mikey never wanted to do it. Please leave him out of it."

Michael inched closer to him and took his hand. "We did it. I went along. I'm so sorry. We'll give you all the pictures we've taken." He started rummaging through the cases and handing over the memory cards from each camera. Finally, he came to one and stopped. "This one is personal. I want to keep it."

"Show it to us or leave it." From her tone, Dasher was tired of being polite. Michael didn't bother to argue.

He shyly smiled and ran a slide show from the digital screen on the back of the camera. They all gasped when they viewed his female persona, who was gorgeous. Delicately boned and completely feminine, she wore a number of different outfits, from elaborate kimonos to rapper gear. In some she appeared childlike.

"What's her name?" Kate had seen drag queens, in fact some who appeared as likenesses of herself. This one was very well done.

Smiling and dropping his eyes, Michael said, "Mei-Lee."

Denny softly whistled. "Well, Chaz, I can see the attraction. She's hot."

He stared dreamily. "So is he." Michael hugged him.

"So, can we take this card with us?" Kate could tell that Michael was holding his breath.

"Yes, but I want to double-check the cases." Denny rooted around but came up empty.

Michael whispered something to Chaz, and Chaz squeezed his knee. "Listen, we're pretty sure Joe Alder is still involved in some shady stuff. Once, we made a delivery to his office late at night and saw some very scary dudes drinking with him. We took our money and got the hell out of there."

Greta, who had been silent, nodded and said, "I'm sure what they say is true."

Watching her, Dasher said, "Greta, when we were at the directors' dinner you handled him with such ease. You told me you had dealt with men like him before. Do you actually know him?"

Overwhelming sadness filled her eyes and made Kate want to hold her. But Dasher was already on the way. She took her hand and all were silent. The gentle act of kindness made Kate love Dasher more.

Greta said, "I saw the film clip that Dasher told me about because Joe decided to send me a copy, too. I was thirteen, alone and starving on the streets in Russia. I was brought to the USA as an 'adopted' child by a couple, but really I was their slave, in every way. They made several movies with various men. Sex for food, you get the understanding."

The contents of Kate's stomach were threatening to rebel. She saw the same expression on everyone's face. Horror and revulsion, but more than that, compassion.

Thankfully, the pizza and beer arrived, and Kate immediately said, "I'll get it."

Denny raised her hand to stop Kate. "No. If someone recognizes you, we're all screwed. I'll get it."

She dug money from her pocket and stuffed it into the delivery boy's hand as the rest of them stretched or walked around the room.

Kate knew that now wasn't the time to lose her cool. She passed beer and napkins around and they quietly continued their discussion, but with a decidedly less hostile bent toward Chaz and Michael.

Greta continued in a monotone. "One of the men in those films was Joe Alder. In fact, since it was in his possession, perhaps it was him in the one he sent us. I've blanked a lot of that time out of my memory and was heavily drugged anyway. He took a special liking to me. He must have recognized me, all grown up and filled out. Not his style, really, a fully developed woman. But he wants to control me again. For his own gain, I know."

Looking directly at Kate, she said, "Along with the video he demanded that I fire Dasher and sign with him. That's why I'm here. To tell Dasher I have to go."

"You'd work for Joe?" Kate couldn't believe it. She considered Greta one of the strongest women she'd ever met.

"Never. I'm leaving, disappearing. I've had an escape plan for years. Saved cash, an account in Switzerland under a different name, even the name of a plastic surgeon to change how I look. I'll die before I go back to him, to them."

"Greta, how did you get away when you were a child?" Kate was trying to put it all together.

"Ha. I walked away. By then I was fifteen and only good for work and keeping the younger ones in line. Then I lived on the streets, much easier in U.S. than Russia, wear clothes from the church bins, save every penny to buy fake identification. I work on films and get discovered by Dasher." The expression on her face changed from sadness to fierce pride.

"Now I could afford really good false papers. But I was also able to have my face, mostly my nose, changed. That was good because it was broken several times. And I got perfect American teeth." She flashed them for the group and they certainly were white.

Denny breathed, "Jesus."

Jock asked, "Why didn't he come after you before, if he recognized you?"

"Because I recognized *him*. I can tie him to child pornography. But now he seems to think he's got all the chippies on his deck."

After exchanging a look with Chaz, Michael said, "Look, if it helps, we did stick around that night and took pictures of the guys leaving his place. We'll give them to you." He dug around and ripped out the padded bottom of a case and produced the card. Denny glared at him and he shrugged.

"We'll do anything else we can, just name it." He and Chaz both looked sincere.

Jock produced a flash drive from her shirt pocket and held it up. "A few of the Elysium members have discreetly hacked his—well, everything of Joe Alder and several of his aliases. He has money in a bunch of places that, according to the IRS, he's never declared. We can turn him in for tax evasion, if nothing else."

If Dasher was surprised by the information she didn't show it. She quickly said, "Before we do, he has to release Kate from her contract. Greta, if you feel you need to go, I understand. But with your help, we might be able to make it safe for you to stay and get Kate out, too."

She smiled sadly. "Of course. I haven't told my *liubov*, my dear Jason, about my past. I at least owe him that before I go. Who knows? It may make my leaving easy."

Dasher gazed across the room at Kate and smiled. "Or it may make it impossible."

CHAPTER EIGHTEEN

Tonight was the big night, on so many levels that Laurel and Stefanie couldn't keep track. The final week before the opening of the hotel had been a blur of last-minute details and planning. The additional preparations for their scheme to trap Joe Alder had been layered on top of everything else, and no one complained.

A few of the Elysium members were among the workers, adding some finishing touches to one of the smaller rooms off the main ballroom. It was reassuring to see them there. The entire crew had been working eighteen-hour days, and Kate had joined them three days before.

Kate invited Joe Alder to the gala and he eagerly accepted because it was a hot-ticket item and, he thought, his crowning moment. He demanded Kate stay clear of Dasher until that night. He had also directed Greta not to drop Dasher as her agent until the night of the party. He obviously thought his plan was coming together perfectly, and his hatred of Dasher blinded him to anything more than his anticipation of crushing her.

Greta made a quick and painful trip to Arizona to tell Jason the truth about her past, and he was so upset with Alder they were afraid he'd blow the whole deal by trying to rip

Joe's throat out before they could spring the trap. Greta was ecstatic that he'd reacted that way. Kate suspected that no man had ever cared for her the way Jason did.

Finally, after Greta talked and pleaded with him at length, and Stefanie and Laurel threatened to have him banned from the event, Jason was on board. He would be Kate's escort. Joe was enjoying that part, too, because he had let Greta know that Jason would no longer be in her future. He was probably looking forward to a wonderful evening of playing dungeon master.

Dasher had purchased disposable cell phones for Greta, Jason, Kate, and herself. She confessed that she felt like a paranoid idiot, but she wasn't about to take a chance. Her future with Kate was riding on the way this night went. With the anonymous cell phones, at least they could talk to each other without worrying about being overheard.

Every night before the opening they called and brought each other up to date. Dasher went about her business and stayed in touch with the other plan details through Jock or Denny. She met secretly with Chaz and Michael twice to map out their part. Today they'd held a brief dress rehearsal to make sure everyone knew where to go and what to do, and to run a final equipment check.

Alder told Chaz and Michael to get into the event, no matter how they had to do it. He wanted them to photograph Dasher and Jason when they got the good news. Chaz assured Joe he had an "in" and left it at that. Chaz was scared to death because Michael had been assigned a risky role, but Michael insisted he could do it. He told Kate and Dasher that Mei-Lee would be honored.

Laurel and Stefanie had been working with Elysium members to nail down the other details. The connections that these women had, both legal and, as they said, extralegal, amazed them. A team of three would be working in Los Angeles while the event was occurring. Although all were curious about who the "three" were, they agreed that the less they knew, the better.

By nine o'clock the gala was in high gear: champagne was flowing, and the hors d'oeuvres were plentiful. Dignitaries from San Francisco, Los Angeles, Sacramento, and even Washington, DC, turned out. Many of the women were members of Elysium, but no one but the other members knew that.

Dasher and Greta watched from the security room, waiting until the right time to join the party. Kate arrived wearing a stunning gown that was all but transparent, and the crowd was appreciative. She was on the arm of Jason, who wore his tuxedo beautifully but seemed to have lockjaw. He plastered a smile on his face and seemed to be searching the crowd.

Dasher saw Laurel elbow Stefanie to go calm Jason down. He appeared to be distracted, probably with worry about Greta. Dasher could relate. Stefanie, wearing a graphite-colored woman's tux by Armani, tailored to fit her larger breasts, walked over and gave him a big hug, probably noting his wooden posture as she held him in her arms.

She whispered something in his ear and Dasher guessed it was about breathing, because she saw his body relax a bit and he pulled back to look at her. "Okay, thanks, sis." Dash could read the words on his lips from ten feet away.

Taking Kate's arm, he laughed with her about something and they proceeded to the ballroom. Stef and Laurel kept working the room, checking details and greeting guests. Dasher was scanning the entrance.

Five minutes later Joe Alder and his date, evidently the

woman he had been trying to transform into Kate through plastic surgery and implants, swept in. Joe still looked like a sweaty pig, though a sweaty pig in a tux. Dasher found herself pitying the woman he brought with him. She was at least ten years younger than Kate and so painfully thin that her fake breasts didn't go with her frame. Dasher had thought her appearance odd before, but now she found it disturbing.

Joe waved at Kate and she must not have bothered to hide her granite-eyed expression when she saw him. He was chuckling at the glare and waved to Jason, too. Kate must have felt Jason's biceps tighten because she yanked gently on him. He turned his head away from Joe and faced her. Whatever he said, Kate nodded her agreement. Dasher found Greta and they made their entrance moments later. The attention was on Greta, for which Dasher was grateful. Greta was smiling, signing autographs, ignoring both Alder and Jason, and looked like she was enjoying every minute. Dasher admired the focus it must have taken to carry off her role.

Dasher stared at Kate for a long while. This was the scenario they had rehearsed and the only part of the plan that allowed her to stay sane. As if she could have done anything else but look at Kate. Then she caught sight of Joe Alder watching as he laughed and chomped faster on his ever-present unlit cigar. She could tell he loved every minute of her performance.

Chaz and Mei-Lee entered the room and Joe immediately lost interest in Dasher and his own date, for that matter. Dash turned and was impressed to see that Mei-Lee had made herself look like a young teen. Chaz was nervously patting her hand. When he caught sight of Joe, Joe motioned them over and overtly flirted with Mei-Lee.

Michael played the part of a shy teen flawlessly. She ducked her head, stood awkwardly, and played with her hair. Joe was practically drooling. Chaz introduced her as his brother's daughter, then excused himself to get them something to drink, only once glancing furtively over his shoulder. Joe evidently told his date to get lost, too, because within a minute he was talking to Mei-Lee by himself.

She giggled and batted her eyelashes at him, dusting an imaginary speck from his ill-fitting jacket. He gestured toward a door in the corner of the ballroom and took her arm, propelling her in that direction.

Stefanie swore as he hurried toward the wrong room. Suddenly Denny, dressed in a silver gown that fit her tall frame like a second skin, and Jock, who had on a gorgeous woman's tux, were at that door, snuggling close to each other. Mei-Lee said something and they changed their course, Joe shrugging and laughing amiably with her, but staring contemptuously at the couple as they walked by.

Once Mei-Lee had him inside the correct room, Stefanie started monitoring the live feed from the room on her cell phone, and Laurel signaled the small group to gather outside the door. Chaz was right behind Kate, beads of sweat on his forehead. Bouncing on the balls of his feet, he said, "We have to get in there. No telling what he'll do if he finds out she's a man."

"Wait, Chaz. Almost ready." Stef watched the screen intently, held up three fingers, then two, then one. "Go!"

Laurel slid her master card key through the lock and they spilled into the room. On cue, Mei-Lee turned to the camera, yanking off her wig and top, revealing herself as a man.

Joe Alder evidently forgot that his pants were around his ankles as his mouth flew open, the cigar dropping to the floor. His penis deflated, but not before the special high-quality camera placed high on the wall next to the door caught the entire scene.

Joe screamed, "What the fuck are you doing in here? Get out!"

Greta boldly stepped forward. "Why, Joe. I didn't know you were gay. Interesting."

Looking completely confused he stuttered, "What are you talking about? I'm not some fucking fag." He seemed to notice Mei-Lee as Michael for the first time. "What the fuck?"

Greta growled, "What's the matter, Joe? Isn't he young enough for you?"

His face started to turn a nasty color of red. "You. I'll have that fucking video of you going viral in another hour."

Dasher stood beside her. "Maybe you should pull up your pants before you do that. There's really not all that much to see."

While wrestling his pants to his waist Joe growled, "I'll ruin both of you. Watch me."

"I think we've watched enough. Just remember, if that video goes on the Internet, so does the one we just took of you having sex with a man. That ought to go over well with your business associates."

Joe's eyes showed surprise but his mouth twisted malevolently. He fumbled for his cell phone in his jacket pocket and finally held it up. "All I have to do is press this button and I send my computer the instruction to release Greta's video. I planned to have you watching anyway."

Holding up her own phone, Dasher said, "Tell you what, we'll do it together. You release yours and I'll release the one we just took of you and your boyfriend. Ready? Set? Go!"

"Wait!" After a beat Joe yelled, "You bitch!" and pressed the button on his phone.

He watched the screen go blank and started swearing. "What did you do?"

Kate had been waiting for this moment. "All of your files

are gone, Joe. Everything on your hard drive, any films you had hidden, they're all gone."

"You can't..." He started stabbing at his phone with no success.

"Even if you have something stored in a place we haven't found, every time it appears on the Internet, it will be deleted and the video of you and your friend will be inserted. The marvels of the electronic age. Wonderful, yes?"

"You can kiss your career good-bye, Hoffman. I'll make sure you never work in this town again."

A deep baritone rumbled from the back of the room. "You're such a cliché, Joe. And about that." On cue the group parted to reveal Jerry Pate with Mimi on his arm. And although he attempted to gently hand her to Dasher and Kate, she stayed by his side.

Looking handsome and distinguished in his tuxedo, he pulled a set of papers from his inside coat pocket, three sheets at the most. "This is a statement releasing Kate Hoffman from her contract with you. Sign it."

The expression on Joe's face transformed from confusion to disbelief to refusal in two seconds. Kate held her breath. This part meant the most to her and Dasher, and it was up to Jerry to carry it off.

Now he and Joe were squaring off. Joe looked ready for a fight.

"I don't have to sign a fucking thing. Hoffman is mine. That dyke you call a daughter will never get Kate."

Before anyone could move, Mimi Pate reached out and slapped Joe so hard his jaw seemed to wobble on his face. "Don't you ever, ever say another thing about our daughter again." Her handprint clearly visible on his face, he simply stared.

Kate glanced at Dasher. Simultaneously they stepped up

to Mimi and each took an arm to stand protectively beside her. She was trembling, but had a grim smile on her lips. Kate then watched in amazement as Jerry seemed to grow in size, if that were possible.

Jerry took a few steps toward Joe. "If you ever want to get one of your so-called clients into a film again, you'll sign this now."

Joe backed up but scoffed, "Pate, there are other stunt assholes besides you in LA."

"Yes, and every one of them will refuse to work on any film that signs an actor represented by you. That's worth millions to any production company."

Joe stared. "If I don't sign, that means you'd screw Hoffman, too, because she's my client." He was sneering but the sweat was pouring off him.

Kate squeezed Mimi's arm and released it, stepping beside Jerry. "I don't care anymore, Joe. I'll be with Dasher no matter what you do."

"You've always been a stupid cunt, Kate. That so-called agent won't be able to find you any movies if your contract is—"

Dasher was on Joe before he finished. She smacked his face and kneed him, doubling him over. Before she could bring both hands down on the back of his head, her father dragged her off and held her, Kate clutching Mimi to keep her upright.

As Joe wheezed and tried to catch his breath, Kate said, "You aren't listening. I said I'll be with Dasher. Period."

The red on Joe Alder's face was turning darker, and Kate couldn't tell which had angered him more: the damage the Pate women had inflicted or the ultimatum Jerry had given him.

"Sign it. She's lost to you anyway. If you take it to court, it'll be tied up for years. Kate's willing to refuse to work."

Fuming, Joe's eyes darted around the small gathering in the room and he spied Greta. "Then I want to trade Kate for Greta. I get Greta."

Pulling herself free from her father, Dasher straightened her suit coat. "Greta makes her own decisions, Joe."

Looking threatening, he demanded, "Greta, come."

Greta slid her hand into the crook of Jason's arm. "I'm not a dog, Joe. I'll never sign with you. But here's what I will do. I have in my possession photos of you with some of your 'associates,' as I remember you always called them. They wouldn't appreciate them being shared with anyone else, like, maybe the authorities."

For the first time Kate saw hesitation on Joe's face. "You wouldn't dare. They'd kill you."

"No. They'd kill *you*." Greta flashed her perfect American smile at Joe.

Joe started toward her, and Kate heard Jason mutter, "Thank you," just before he smashed his fist into Joe's face and dropped him to his knees. Shaking his hand, he turned to the crowd and grinned. "Self-defense."

Kate said, "That's the way I saw it."

The others all nodded vigorously. Jerry Pate was the only one who checked on Alder.

Ember quickly appeared and handed a bar towel to Alder. Looking around she said to Stefanie, "Didn't want him to bleed on the new carpet." Then she glanced at Jason's hand and added, "I'll get some ice."

As she hustled out of the room Kate remarked, "I hope you're planning to give that woman a raise. She's everywhere."

Greta was looking at Jason like he'd just invented chocolate. He returned the expression with pure adoration.

Kate watched Laurel gazing at them and smiling, and when she caught Laurel's eye, she winked.

"Is there a back door from this room?" Dasher had her phone out and was quietly talking on it.

Jock said, "Sure is. The service hall is right on the other side of this wall." She tapped a panel in two places and it slid to the side. "Tell them to meet us at the loading dock."

Only mildly fretting, Kate asked, "Where are you taking him? Is cement involved?"

Jerry Pate and Dasher hefted the semiconscious Alder to his feet. Dasher seemed to consider Kate's question, then grinned at her. "That's tempting. Actually, we've been in touch with some Treasury agents who have questions for Joe. Although I didn't send the video, I did tip the feds to look into some of the aliases I provided. I don't know how, but an anonymous person e-mailed quite a bit of information to me. I felt it my duty to share it with them."

With Jock leading the way, the four of them disappeared out the service door, which slid noiselessly back in place once they were gone. Ember materialized with a champagne bucket full of ice for Jason's hand.

Stef examined the hand, already swelling considerably, and said she thought a few knuckles were busted.

Jason groaned. "It looks so easy in the movies."

❖

The gala continued until two in the morning, with Kate and Greta sharing the star duties. Both of them stood on the stage, arms around each other's waist, and waved to the guests, taking turns welcoming them and pointing out the amenities of the hotel, as well as toasting the women of Hotel Liaison.

"And I'd like to thank my new agent, Dasher Pate, for

introducing me to Greta. I know she has a bright future and I'm honored to be her friend."

The applause was polite, and though most guests neither knew nor cared who anyone's agent was, Kate and Greta, and Dasher, had tears in their eyes.

As soon as Jason returned from the emergency room, Greta whisked him away to her room. Next came Kate and Laurel's parents, who thankfully had been taken over by the Pates.

Kate had been so relieved when the elevator doors closed on the Pates and the Hoffmans, taking them to their rooms. She was grateful that they seemed to have hit it off.

On their way up in the Elysium lift, Dasher said, "How do you think your parents took your announcement?"

Kate grinned. "About my change of agents? Or the fact that I'm in love with you?"

"Ah, I'm guessing it was the love statement. Your mother still hadn't blinked by the time we said good night."

"I noticed. I think your mom will take her under her wing. Daddy was thrilled to have Jerry Pate as, how did he say it? Oh, yes, a member of the family."

Dasher glanced at her questioningly. "Yeah, sounded like he thinks our relationship is permanent."

Kate took her hand and together they entered the room. Once inside, Kate pushed Dasher's jacket off her shoulders to land on the floor and they shared a long, slow kiss. "Is that okay with you? Permanent?"

Gazing lovingly into her eyes, Dasher said, "It's everything I've ever wanted. It's all I want. You."

Kate's body responded immediately to Dasher's words. "It's odd. I feel so free now, like someone has lifted a crushing weight from my shoulders. I've never been so sure about anything."

She began unbuttoning Dash's shirt, nipping along the line of her jaw, caressing her breasts through the fabric. Dasher gasped at the touch.

"Dasher, I never knew that taking the risk to be myself would allow all my dreams to come true."

Gazing into Kate's eyes, Dasher whispered, "And all of mine."

Chapter Nineteen

Life had changed dramatically for Kate during the three months since the party. The tabloids had gone nuts over Joe Alder's arrest by the Treasury agents, and rumors were flying around the industry about him.

As Kate read various articles, she found out she wasn't the only one disgusted with Joe. Many, probably emboldened by his almost certain long-time incarceration, said they thought he was connected to the mob. And more than a few of them expressed relief to have him gone from the scene.

Personally, Kate was ecstatic. With Dasher as her agent, she was getting offers for real films, some of them independent, some from huge studios. Even the adventure thrillers involved strong roles for the women. Whether they kept coming or not, she wouldn't have to play the big-breasted bimbo again.

She and Dasher had become an item in the gossip rags. Most accused one or both of them, mostly Kate, of using the other to further her own career. The accusations bothered Kate. A lot. The questions she was constantly peppered with always insinuated that she was either a conniving bitch or that seeing Dasher was just another fling.

After all, she'd gone through all of the Hollywood hunky men. It would only be natural to add the hot butch Dasher Pate to her list. Was that how she got Dasher to represent her? Who was next?

Dasher seemed to take all the commotion in stride, and every moment they spent together Kate fell more deeply in love with her. She'd never experienced the intensity of their connection, the intimacy. Their sexual relationship was so visceral, she couldn't get enough of Dasher. They were passionate, playful, adventurous, even sweet. Kate never imagined she could feel this way about another being.

Yet Dasher had read the articles, too. And as close as they were, she seemed to be waiting for the other shoe to drop. She let Kate take the lead, as though she didn't trust her to be there the next day.

At moments in their lovemaking, especially when they held each other afterward, Kate was sure Dasher was crying, but she knew better than to ask her why. *She* was the reason. No matter how much Kate tried to reassure Dasher, the fear of her leaving lingered. The movie business and Dasher's personal past had made it almost impossible for her to trust that someone could love her unconditionally.

With each day, Kate was surer she wanted to be that person. No amount of fame, no amount of money, no amount of approval of the masses measured up to the way she felt about Dasher. Nothing matched the light in Dasher's face when she saw Kate, nor the way Kate's heart flipped when Dash entered the room.

❖

Kate was the maid of honor in Stef and Laurel's wedding at the Hotel Liaison. Dasher had opted to be an usher, saying something about handling desiccated rats before stuffing herself in a dress. They'd flown up two days earlier on a private plane chartered by Dasher because the paparazzi were becoming as thick as flies at a picnic.

Kate decided that from now on, they were taking a private jet. At least she could be herself with Dash. She wanted to be openly affectionate and despised some of the ugly comments that she had read recently on blogs, social Web sites, and the media. Oh, the encouraging ones far outnumbered them, but how could people be so self-righteous, so judgmental? What gave them the right?

Most of these idiots assured her that when her fling with Dasher ended and she was married to a *man*, they would eventually forgive her. The idea of ever being apart from Dasher sickened her. Those people would never have the kind of love she had with Dash, because they were incapable of it. Well, that wasn't her problem.

Her problem was convincing Dasher that what they had was real. Dasher had to be able to trust her to be there for her. Dasher had to trust that her heart was safe in Kate's keeping. Kate wasn't sure she could do that, because she'd never done it before. What would it take to make Dasher believe?

❖

"You look beautiful, Laurel. It's really true what they say about brides, isn't it?" Kate was admiring Laurel's stunning dress and the joy so evident on her face. Marilyn Hoffman was fussing back and forth between Kate and Laurel, adjusting this and that.

"It certainly is. Laurel, you look radiant. I'm so happy. Stefanie is perfect for you. Even your brother Teddy is here. Isn't that wonderful?"

Kate and Laurel exchanged glances. Ted was there because he and his family had gotten a free ride on a Beresford corporate jet and he was trying to social climb with Stefanie's family. He'd sent his wife and two boys on a sightseeing trip during the wedding. Wouldn't want to broaden their tiny little minds with a same-sex marriage.

"Yeah, Mom, just great. Say, maybe you should go check on everyone, make sure they're in their seats." Laurel looked like she was on the edge with their mom.

Kate said, "I think Daddy may talk Jerry Pate's ear off, Mom. Maybe you could herd him away for a minute or two."

Shaking her head, Marilyn flipped a wrist. "Oh, your father has already arranged to sit with him and Mimi at the reception dinner. We've actually become friends with both of them."

Casting an appraising eye on Kate, something that always made Kate brace for the next comment, she said, "Kate, is something bothering you?"

Now both her mother and Laurel studied her. Her mother asked, "Is it something to do with Dasher? Oh, my, you aren't going to dump her, are you, dear? I do so like the Pates, and she's completely in love with you."

Kate and Laurel were suddenly staring in disbelief at their mother. Kate whispered, "You approve of Dasher?"

A sharp rap on the door and then Dasher was standing there, gorgeous in the most elegant Sonia Rykiel suit Kate had ever seen. Stef and Dasher had shopped for their clothes together and wouldn't tell the sisters what they were wearing. After studying each of them, Dasher said, "What?"

Laurel was first to recover. "Nothing, Dasher. Are we ready?"

Although an eyebrow of suspicion briefly registered on Dasher's face, she said, "The Hoffmans look stunning today, especially you, Laurel." When her mother shifted her attention to Laurel, Dasher gave Kate a heart-stopping expression that told her she was the most beautiful creature in the universe to one Dasher Pate.

Laurel quickly said, "Hey, Dasher, would you take Mom and seat her? Thanks."

Again with the eyebrow, but Dasher dutifully offered her arm to Mrs. Hoffman and Marilyn actually tittered a bit as they walked out the door. The quick backward glance from Dash told Kate and Laurel that she didn't mind at all.

Closing the door, Kate faced Laurel. "Okay, are you ready to marry Stefanie Beresford? For better or worse? From this day forward? No matter what the freak happens?"

Grinning, Laurel said, "I can't wait."

Tears sprang to Kate's eyes and she rushed to hug her sister close. "I'm so happy for you, Laur. You're perfect for each other."

Holding on tight for a few seconds, finally Laurel pulled back. "What about you and Dasher? I don't know how, but Mom seems to like the idea. I guess between Dasher and her parents, and the fact that you're deliriously happy, Mother has had a change of heart."

"Laurel, this is your day. Just yours. We need to go. You shouldn't worry about my problems."

Shaking her gently by the shoulders, Laurel said, "Tell me in one sentence. Now."

Trying not to smudge her makeup with tear trails, Kate said miserably, "Dasher doesn't trust me, Kate. She keeps waiting for me to leave. And I can't blame her. Look at my track record."

"That was more than one sentence, but I get the idea. Kate, is Dasher the one? The only one? Be honest."

"Oh, Kate. She's been the only one since I first met her five years ago. I just was too self-involved to recognize and accept it. But how can I convince her? Even you're skeptical."

Another knock and Kate hugged her and opened the door to reveal their father, all dressed up and smiling at them.

"Okay, ladies, time to get this show on the road."

Ah, Dad. Always the romantic, Kate thought.

As they moved through the hall to the ballroom, Chaz Hockaday appeared and started taking photos. They all stopped and posed for him. Chaz and Michael were making more money these days by covering same-sex weddings than they had been sneaking around trying to capture celebrities in embarrassing situations.

They were even scoring some straight gigs because of Jason and Greta's recommendations. Michael was ecstatic, and even Chaz seemed very pleased with himself. Mei-Lee was his date for the wedding.

Chaz and Michael were the only photographers allowed into the ceremony. The rest of the reporters and media were hovering outside of the hotel, mostly because of the presence of Kate and Greta Sarnoff. Jason was Stefanie's best man.

❖

The wedding went off smoothly, with a good amount of nose blowing and sniffling from the guests. When Kate looked beyond the couple to Dasher just as the minister was declaring them spouses for life, she saw happiness and yearning and sadness, all emotions she'd learned to recognize because of her love for Dasher. When had she become so attuned to another being that she could do that?

She longed to erase the sadness and yearning from Dasher's face forever. Then she focused on Laurel and Stef and knew how she could do it. And perhaps she'd be able to erase her own doubts, too.

With startling clarity she realized that she, too, had been holding back from Dasher. What if Dasher couldn't learn to trust her? What if she would forever, no matter what Kate did, always retain that final piece of herself that doomed Kate to always be on trial?

Kate did have a bad track record, but what if after all she'd risked, Dasher couldn't take the final leap of faith? Dasher's eyes met hers and Kate gave a small smile. Perhaps it wasn't just Dasher who had to take that risk.

❖

Two hours later the dinner had concluded and the dancing was about to begin. Kate toasted the couple, wishing them a long life of wonderful adventures together, while thinking of Dasher the entire time. Jason toasted them and Greta, his bride-to-be, saying he could only hope to have as wonderful a relationship as Stef and Laurel.

Stefanie and Laurel walked to the dance floor and the music began. They waltzed beautifully together, moving fluidly through the steps. For the second dance their parents joined them. About halfway through, Kate stood and strode over and held out her hand to Dasher. She knew all eyes were on them and she didn't care. She was determined, by God, to dance with the woman she loved.

Dasher seemed taken aback that Kate would be so bold, but within seconds the world around them faded and it seemed that only the two of them were moving together as one. As the music changed and others took the floor, Dasher said, "Thank you. That was a dance I'll always remember."

Not yet, but Kate was getting there. Within the next hour the reception was filling the halls with joy. Even Ted Hoffman had asked Stefanie to dance and looked like he was eyeballing Mei-Lee next. Kate decided not to say a word and only hoped Chaz had his camera at the ready.

Kate searched for Dasher in the crowd and found her chatting amiably with Kate's parents. She stood gazing at them until a touch to her elbow pulled her from her reverie. When she turned, Stefanie stood there with a serious look on her face.

"What's wrong?"

"Well, I'm sorry to say that the reporters are getting a bit restless. They heard about you dancing with Dasher and are practically ready to storm the doors. Twitter can be a pain at times." Stef looked a bit harried.

"Greta tried to distract them, but her engagement to Jason just isn't as titillating as you dating Dasher."

And here was the opportunity Kate had been preparing for. "I'm sorry, Stef. I didn't want any of my stuff to detract from this day for you and Laurel. Where's Dasher?"

"Right behind you. What's up?" She whirled to see a concerned expression on Dasher's beautiful face. Poor Dash, always solving other people's problems. Well, it ended here.

"Come on, we have a fire to either feed or put out, I'm not sure which. Either way, we need to talk to the reporters."

"Oh. Well, I guess the party's over then. Let's go." From the stricken look on Dasher's face, Kate guessed she thought this was the moment Kate would deny her feelings for her. Kate was furious.

She kissed Stefanie's cheek and said, "Leave it to us."

They marched through the lobby, Kate in the lead with Dasher's hand firmly in hers. When she reached the reception desk she looked around and immediately found the media, who had been crowded into the foyer where the photo shoot had been held, just a short time ago. *My, how things have changed*, Kate thought.

Someone shouted in recognition of Kate and she plastered a smile on her face, turned to check out Dasher, and saw trepidation in her eyes. *Here goes*.

Waving hello, they walked over with flashes nearly blinding Kate and, she imagined, Dasher, too. "Hello, ladies and gentlemen, and I use the term loosely." A friendly ripple of laughter went through the group.

"Hey, Kate! Is your agent your date for your sister's wedding?"

Kate knew this was a softball question to warm her up. She understood the game. Chaz and Michael had filled her in on any missing pieces when they'd had dinner with them a few weeks earlier. She glanced around and saw Chaz, who looked nervously at a few of the more feral of his former colleagues.

Squeezing Dasher's hand, she didn't look at her but answered, "She sure is."

"So you need a gay date for the gay wedding?" A few of the reporters snickered.

Taking a breath she said, "I invited who I wanted to invite to the wedding."

There was a brief pause and she knew she'd given them an opening. At this point they were imagining a feeding frenzy.

"So, Dasher Pate is your new toy?"

Ouch. "Cut to the chase, boys and girls. What do you want to know?" She'd played the game so often that she was sick of it. She was through playing.

One of the more aggressive of the group, and a man that Chaz had warned her about, was the first to spit it out. In a taunting tone, he asked, "Are you planning to *marry* Dasher Pate?"

There it was. Kate took a breath and laid it on the line. Looking straight into Dasher's eyes, she said, "I don't know. She hasn't asked."

Shouting broke out after that, with everyone's attention on Dasher to find out more. When Dasher finally was able to calm them down, she opened her mouth, only to find that Kate had slipped away from the group. She furtively looked around and caught a glimpse of Kate's pale peach gown as she disappeared into the Elysium elevator at the end of the bank of elevators. Evidently no one else had seen her escape.

"Dasher! Are you planning to ask Kate Hoffman to marry you?" The same question rebounded throughout the group.

Holding up her hands, Dasher quieted them. When she had their attention she said, "Excuse me."

She glanced at Chaz, who quickly turned his camera toward the group and took a full-flash photo, making them all turn away and protest for a second while Dasher aimed straight for the Elysium elevator. She hid behind the potted plants while they were trying to figure out what had just happened and were texting their news to the various news outlets.

Someone spotted her just as the elevator arrived, and before the door closed he slid into the car with her. It was the same jerk who'd asked Kate about marrying Dasher. Dasher quietly touched a blue button on the panel and endured the brief ride. The intruder was aggressively demanding answers to his questions when the elevator arrived on the Elysium floor, where Dash and Kate's room was located.

One of the young students she knew to be a varsity basketball player at Cal was guarding the door. The man ignored her and tried to step out of the car with Dasher, but the guard stopped him with one hand and held him in the car.

Dasher nodded her thanks to the young woman, who tilted her head in the direction Kate had gone. Dasher watched the elevator doors close on the protesting reporter and the guard. Chuckling at the expression of fury and maybe a touch of trepidation on his face, she went to find Kate.

Letting herself into the darkened room, she saw Kate standing at the window, looking out at the City by the Bay. She walked over and slid her arms around Kate, pulling her into an embrace.

Kate resisted at first, then allowed the contact. They stood quietly for a few minutes. Dasher said, "You might have just thrown your career away down there. Not at first, but over time."

Listlessly, Kate replied, "The rumors have been circulating since you became my agent. What's new?" She had hoped that Dasher would get the hint. She didn't know what else to do. Dasher had to take the risk to love her. Kate couldn't make her.

Dasher's mouth was beside her ear and she kissed it gently. "Kate, will you marry me? Will you spend the rest of your life with me? Will you be my girl?"

There it was. All the missing pieces of Kate tumbled into place and at last she was whole. She turned in Dasher's arms and gazed into the deep gray eyes with flashes of blue in them. She was home.

"Yes. Forever, yes. What took you so long?"

Shyly smiling, Dasher said, "I thought it was your risk to take. I didn't realize I had to take a chance, too."

"So, do we get to set a date?" Kate kissed Dasher's chin and nibbled on her lower lip. Then she slipped her arms around Dasher's neck and pulled her closer to better suck the very soft skin just under her ear.

Dasher growled, "Any time, anywhere, any place. But…"

Kate pulled back to look at her. "But what?"

Dasher reached around to the back of her dress and unzipped it. "We'll set the date tomorrow. Tonight is just you and me, and nothing in between."

Stepping away from Dasher, Kate let her dress drop to the floor and was thrilled with the reaction. Then she shed what undergarments she was wearing and turned toward the bedroom. Glancing over her shoulder, she said, "You'd better not be wearing those clothes when you come to bed. Now."

Hearing buttons pop and material rip as she left the room made her grin. She threw back the covers of the bed and patted the space beside her. "Here, right where you belong."

Dasher was beside her in a heartbeat. Then on top of her. "I love you, Kate. I've been in love with you since we first met."

"I know. Now, I know. I'm in love with you, too, Dash. I always will be."

Then Dasher was inside her, flooding all of her senses with that delicious sensation she'd come to crave. The one only Dasher could give her.

When Kate came to her senses, she looked deeply into Dasher's eyes and saw what she'd hoped to see, and when Dasher thundered to a climax it was Kate's name she called, again and again. Kate knew she was the only one.

Their intimacy held the passion of new love and the certainty of their future together. Kate never knew a bond that strong could exist between two people.

As they lay in each other's arms afterward, Kate thought about what she might have given up for the chance to be with Dasher. She smiled and tucked in closer to Dash.

She'd made the right choice this time. For all the right reasons.

About the Authors

JLee Meyer utilizes her background in psychology and speech pathology in her work as an international communication consultant. Spending time in airports, planes, and hotel rooms allows her the opportunity to pursue two of her favorite passions: reading and writing lesbian fiction.

JLee and her life partner celebrate their lives together in Northern California.

Books Available From Bold Strokes Books

Fever by VK Powell. Hired gun Zakaria Chambers is hired to provide a simple escort service to philanthropist Sara Ambrosini, but nothing is as simple as it seems, especially love. (978-1-60282-135-4)

High Risk by JLee Meyer. Can actress Kate Hoffman really risk all she's worked for to take a chance on love? Or is it already too late? (978-1-60282-136-1)

Missing Lynx by Kim Baldwin and Xenia Alexiou. On the trail of a notorious serial killer, Elite Operative Lynx's growing attraction to a mysterious mercenary could be her path to love—or to death. (978-1-60282-137-8)

Spanking New by Clifford Henderson. A poignant, hilarious, unforgettable look at life, love, gender, and the essence of what makes us who we are. (978-1-60282-138-5)

Magic of the Heart by C.J. Harte. CEO Susan Hettinger and wild, impulsive rock star M.J. Carson couldn't be more different if they tried—but opposites attract in ways neither woman can resist. (978-1-60282-131-6)

Ambereye by Gill McKnight. Jolie Garoul is falling in love with her assistant. The big problem is, Jolie is a werewolf. (978-1-60282-132-3)

Collision Course by C.P. Rowlands. Tragedy leaves Brie O'Malley and Jordan Carter fearful and alone. Can they find the courage to take a second chance on love? (978-1-60282-133-0)

Mephisto Aria by Justine Saracen. Opera singer Katherina Marov's destiny may be to repeat the mistakes of her father when she becomes involved in a dangerous love affair. (978-1-60282-134-7)

Battle Scars by Meghan O'Brien. Returning Iraq war veteran Ray McKenna struggles with the battle scars that can only be healed by love. (978-1-60282-129-3)

Bold Strokes
BOOKS
WEBSTORE
PRINT AND EBOOKS
Romance
Mystery
Intrigue
MATINEE BOOKS
LIBERTY
EDITION
BOLD
STROKES
BOOKS
Adventure
victory
EDITIONS
AEROS
Erotica
Fantasy
Sci-Fi
http://www.boldstrokesbooks.com